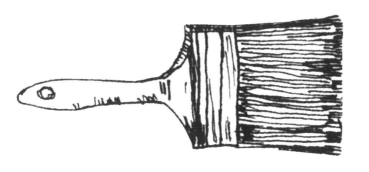

Wicked
Haints

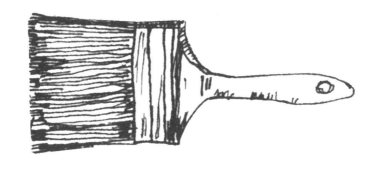

Wicked Haints

A Savannah Ghost Story

JK Bovi

4880 Lower Valley Road • Atglen, PA 19310

Dedication

To Bob

Cover design concept and illustration by JK Bovi

Ouija is a registered trademark of Parker Brothers.

Schiffer Books are available at special discounts for bulk purchases for sales promotions or premiums. Special editions, including personalized covers, corporate imprints, and excerpts can be created in large quantities for special needs. For more information contact the publisher:

Published by Schiffer Publishing Ltd.
4880 Lower Valley Road
Atglen, PA 19310
Phone: (610) 593-1777; Fax: (610) 593-2002
E-mail: Info@schifferbooks.com

For the largest selection of fine reference books on this and related subjects,
please visit our website at
www.schifferbooks.com.
We are always looking for people to write books on new and related subjects.
If you have an idea for a book, please contact us at
proposals@schifferbooks.com.

This book may be purchased from the publisher.
Include $5.00 for shipping.
Please try your bookstore first.
You may write for a free catalog.

In Europe, Schiffer books are distributed by
Bushwood Books
6 Marksbury Ave.
Kew Gardens
Surrey TW9 4JF England
Phone: 44 (0) 20 8392 8585; Fax: 44 (0) 20 8392 9876
E-mail: info@bushwoodbooks.co.uk
Website: www.bushwoodbooks.co.uk

Designed by Mark David Bowyer
Type set in Acadian / Book Antiqua

ISBN: 978-0-7643-4383-4
Printed in the United States of America

Savannah, Georgia

Be mindful where you tread . . . you walk upon Savannah's dead

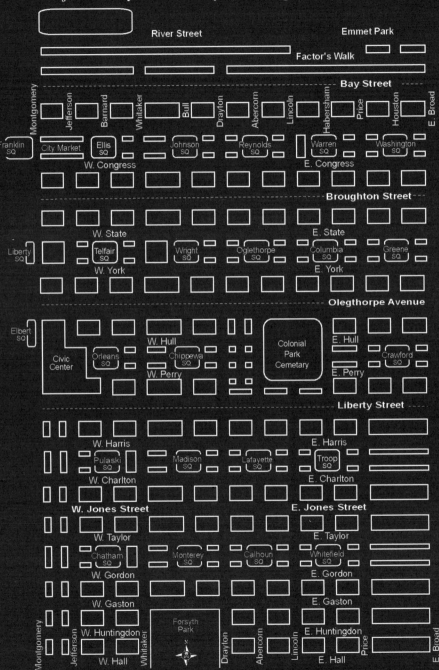

River Street

Emmet Park

Factor's Walk

Bay Street

Montgomery · Jefferson · Barnard · Whitaker · Bull · Drayton · Abercorn · Lincoln · Habersham · Price · Houston · E. Broad

Franklin SQ · City Market · Ellis SQ · Johnson SQ · Reynolds SQ · Warren SQ · Washington SQ

W. Congress — E. Congress

Broughton Street

W. State — E. State

Liberty SQ · Telfair SQ · Wright SQ · Oglethorpe SQ · Columbia SQ · Greene SQ

W. York — E. York

Olegthorpe Avenue

Elbert SQ

Civic Center · Orleans SQ · W. Hull · Chippewa SQ · W. Perry · Colonial Park Cemetary · E. Hull · Crawford SQ · E. Perry

Liberty Street

W. Harris — E. Harris

Pulaski SQ · Madison SQ · Lafayette SQ · Troop SQ

W. Charlton — E. Charlton

W. Jones Street — **E. Jones Street**

W. Taylor — E. Taylor

Chatham SQ · Monterey SQ · Calhoun SQ · Whitefield SQ

W. Gordon — E. Gordon

W. Gaston — E. Gaston

Montgomery · Jefferson · W. Huntingdon · Whitaker · Forsyth Park · Drayton · Abercorn · Lincoln · E. Huntingdon · Price · E. Broad

N

W. Hall — E. Hall

map by jkbovi

Chapter One

Darrel placed his hands on his hips and looked at the front porch of the old house on Jones Street with the critical eye of an experienced house painter. He estimated how much he would charge — $500 for the porch, which included a fresh coat of haint blue on the ceiling. Should be an easy three-day job stretched into a week. No one would expect a person to paint a house in Savannah, Georgia in mid-July in a less amount of time, except maybe someone from the North. He hoped the client was local, but by the sound of her voice on the phone, there could be trouble.

A beige Lexus hesitated at the stop sign and then slipped into the open parking place in front of the house. The engine cut, the car door opened, and a lady stepped out. She slammed the car door and studied the porch, also with a critical eye, but from that of a realtor.

Her high heels clicked on ancient cobblestones as she marched to Darrel.

"Are you the painter?" Miss Realtor asked.

"Yep. *Anything Painted*," he answered and handed her a business card that read:

ANYTHING PAINTED

He was proud of his card, proud of his business, and proud of his name printed in fancy type.

"Cute," she said and shoved the card into her skirt pocket (keeping it in case she needed to sue him for shoddy workmanship). "How much to paint the porch?"

"Six hundred," Darrel said. His price went up on account of the Lexus.

She hid her smile and remained stone faced. He was more than cheap, he was dirt cheap. She was used to dealing with service people on Hilton Head Island and their prices were way out of reasonable. She was going to enjoy handling rental properties in Savannah. "How much to paint the *back* porch?" she asked.

"I didn't look at the back porch."

"Come take a look," she said, stomping up the steps. Her heels clicked across the heart pine boards to the entrance. She shoved the key into the lock, turned it quick, and pushed the door open. Stepping inside, she seemed to disappear into the golden afternoon sun that poured through the parlor windows.

Darrel peeked in. It was a wonderfully bright home, vacant of furnishings, but filled with warmth and happiness. He envisioned laughing children playing on the parlor floor, while the mother of the house baked a pie in the kitchen, and somewhere, in a distant room, the father read *The Savannah Morning News*.

"Well come in," she said from the kitchen.

"Yes ma'am." Darrel wiped his shoes on the doormat and stepped into the three-bedroom house on Jones Street. He walked down the narrow hallway, past the parlor on the right, and the downstairs closet renovated into a bathroom on the left. He entered the modern kitchen as she unlocked the back door.

Darrel wanted to slow down to admire the new white cabinets, imported granite counters, stainless steel appliances, Art-deco lighting fixtures and faucets, but the realtor held open the back door to hurry him along.

Stepping onto the back porch, instead of looking at what needed to be painted, he was mesmerized by the beauty of the backyard. There was nothing as lovely as a secluded garden in an old Savannah home. Ivy had been winding its way up the brick

walls for over a hundred years. The flowers were in bloom and the air was sweet with their fragrance. In a corner there was a stone bench beneath a large, live oak. Spanish moss on the tree's huge knurled branches added to the garden's enchanting, mysterious appearance.

She jingled the house keys and asked, "So how much?"

Darrel walked the length of the porch. He looked over the railing, studied the boards under his feet and when he looked up at the ceiling he saw the familiar color of haint blue. "Five hundred for the back porch."

"Does that price include paint?"

"Nope. Paint is extra."

"How much for the paint?"

"Depends on what you want."

"I want white."

"White?"

"Yes. Do you have a problem with that?"

"No ma'am; I'll paint it any color you want."

"How much for the paint?"

Darrel did some quick math in his head. "Two hundred for the paint."

"That's ridiculous. What kind of paint are you using?"

"The good stuff," Darrel said with a smile.

"Fine. I don't care what paint you use, but I don't want to see any other color coming through. Do you hear me?"

"You want me to paint over the haint blue on the ceilings?" Darrel asked in surprise.

"Of course I do. I said I want everything white."

"I will have to put at least two, maybe three coats to cover up the haint blue. You sure you want me to do that?"

"So you're telling me it will cost more for paint than what you just told me?" Her voice indicated annoyance.

Darrel leaned against the porch post and looked up at the vast expanse of light blue over their heads. He thought it looked like a wide river of brilliant peaceful water. If a person looked long enough and hard enough, it might appear the water was moving, flowing over their heads.

She jingled the house keys again and tapped her pointed heels on the heart pine floorboards.

"I'm just saying maybe you don't want to paint over the haint blue. That's all."

"Why not?"

Darrel wanted a cigarette. He was no longer in the mood to educate the ignorant. She might be from Hilton Head, South Carolina, and some people up that way *knew* about the low country, but some people did not. She must have moved down from the North to take advantage of the real estate boom in the early nineties. Houses were bought, flipped, and sold at alarming rates. Money came fast and easy. Work was plentiful, and a good painter had more than enough to keep busy.

That was then. This was now.

Now Miss Realtor was scrambling to make money by renting homes owned by those who could no longer sell them for a decent profit. She was a bottom feeder. Darrel called people like her *mud minnows*. They stole your fishing bait.

"Some people around here think haint blue keeps the evil spirits out. Don't they use that color on Hilton Head?" Darrel asked.

"Most people in Hilton Head are wealthy and educated. They don't believe in low country superstitions."

Darrel *really* wanted a cigarette. There was a time when he would have refused to paint over haint blue because he, like many others, understood the reason for the homeowner having painted the porch ceilings haint blue in the first place. There was an unwanted spirit lurking somewhere nearby who wanted to get into the house.

Times were different now, though. Jobs were hard to come by. The payment on his trailer was past due.

She tapped her foot on the heart pineboards, unaware of the value and importance of antique heart pine. It took 500 years for heart pine to mature enough to be used for construction. The trees once dominated the southern coast of Georgia. Now there were only 10,000 acres left.

"You interested in the job or not?" she asked.

"Yes ma'am. Not a problem. I'll paint both porches white, if that's what you want."

"That's what I want. Write me up an estimate."

"Yes ma'am, I'll get the paperwork out of my truck." He walked through the house without looking into the pleasant rooms. He knew the house would not be a happy place much longer and he did not want to acknowledge his part in the deal.

Chapter Two

Darrel sat behind the steering wheel in the front seat of his truck, smoked a cigarette, and wrote his estimate with a broken pencil. The door was open. A shadow fell over him, and when he looked up, Miss Realtor looked back.

"How do you want to get paid?" she asked.

"A check will be fine," he answered, handing her the estimate and cupping the cigarette in his hand. Some people did not like cigarette smoke. His mother raised him to be polite and his father had reinforced it with a smack against the back of his head.

She rolled her eyes and took the paper. "I will pay you half now and the other half when the job is finished." She clicked her way across the cobblestones to her Lexus. Opening the door, she climbed in, turned the engine on, closed the door, and sat in her air-conditioned car to write the check.

Darrel sucked on the cigarette and looked at the front porch. It was a shame to paint over the haint blue. It was an unusually pretty shade. Someone had taken considerable care in selecting just the perfect color.

Thomas had been walking around the block. He was on his third go-round when he noticed Darrel sitting in the old brown Ford truck. He saw the lady in her car writing and thought it would be safe to approach his friend. Much like a stealthy marsh bird, Thomas leaned in to ask, "Did you get the job?"

"Yep."

Thomas was all smiles. What was good for Darrel was good for him. Sometimes he worked for Darrel and this would be one of those times. There would be a paycheck this week and that was nice.

Thomas was a Bethesda Boy. The Bethesda Orphanage was established in seventeen forty-something by Reverend Whitefield and it was the oldest orphanage in America. Thomas was just one of the thousands of boys who had walked out of the home with a good education, a sense of importance, and a good religious upbringing. Honest, moral, and of reputable character, he needed very little to be satisfied with his life: an honest day's work, a good fishing hole, and a roof over his head made him a happy man.

Darrel stepped out of his truck and said, "We're going to paint the front and back porches."

"That right? How much ya get?"

Darrel showed him the estimate. Thomas raised his eyebrows and grinned. He was genuinely happy for his friend.

"What color?" Thomas asked.

"White."

"All of it?"

"Yep. All white. Both porches."

"What about the haint blue?"

"It's gonna be white."

Thomas shook his head, looked at his old paint splattered sneakers, and said, "Well that just ain't right. Nope, that just ain't right," he mumbled. He didn't care what Darrel did, but he certainly was not going to be the one to paint over the haint blue. He was a God-fearing man and messing with dead souls and disgruntled spirits was not something he wanted any part of. Nope.

Miss Realtor left the car engine running, swung her legs out, slammed the door, and marched across the cobblestones to Darrel and Thomas.

Thomas politely smiled, stepped back, and, like a swamp critter, seeming to fade into his environment.

"Who is he?" she asked.

"Oh, that's Thomas. He helps me sometimes."

"When will this job be done?" she asked.

"Two, maybe three days," he lied. He looked up at the clear Savannah sky.

She looked at the sky. Thomas looked at the sky.

"Might rain," Darrel said.

She handed him the check. He took it, carefully folded it in half, and then gingerly put it in his shirt pocket.

Hesitating for a moment, she looked at Thomas and handed Darrel the keys to the house on Jones Street.

"That isn't necessary ma'am," he said, not wanting any added responsibility.

"Take the house keys. You might need to get inside," she said, wondering where outdoor painters went to the bathroom. She certainly did not want the neighbors complaining about strange men peeing on their bushes.

Darrel took the keys and shoved them into his back pocket.

"Call me when the job is done."

"Yes ma'am."

"Don't take too long. I want this place rented by the end of the month."

"Yes ma'am."

She clicked across the cobblestones, opened her car door, climbed inside, turned out of the parking space, and drove into the path of a tour trolley.

The guide was speaking over a microphone to the tourists. "Some folks round here think haint blue keeps the ghosts out of the house, which is important when you live in a town like Savannah that was built on top its dead. The color haint blue, ain't blue, ain't

green.....damnit lady!!!" The driver slammed on the brakes and stopped in mid-sentence.

The tourists jerked forward, their mouths open with surprise, as they shot out-of-focus pictures with their cameras. (Some would return to wherever they came from, look back at their shots to see streaks of lights and shadows in the pictures they took in front of the little white house with the haint blue porch ceiling on Jones Street. They would tell their friends the haze was a ghost. Only a few people would believe it. Their friends would also find it difficult to believe how nice the trolley driver was to the crazy lady who they almost hit when she pulled out in front of them.)

Sam the driver leaned out the tour trolley window. "You okay ma'am?"

She rolled down her window. "Sorry. I didn't see you."

Darrel and Thomas hid amused smiles. How could you *not* see a big white trolley?

"You go ahead ma'am and drive careful now."

"Oh, it was my mistake; you go first."

"No ma'am, I insist; a southern gentleman will always wait for a lady."

"Thank you," she said and sped down Jones Street to disappear around the corner.

Sam, unfazed by the driver in the fancy car, continued with his tour-talk, "In Savannah, there are some folks who fear out-of-state drivers almost as much as the ghosts."

He waved to Darrel and Thomas as he passed.

Darrel and Thomas waved back and then climbed into Darrel's truck. Their windows were open. The air conditioner had stopped working quite some time back.

"We going to get paint?" Thomas asked.

16

"Naw. We'll do that in the morning. I was thinking of getting a drink."

Thomas smiled in agreement.

"Lets go to Pinkie Master's. Ya know Jimmie Carter announced he was going to run for president there," Darrel said and drove down Jones Street — without hitting a tour trolley.

"You don't say. President Jimmie Carter, huh?" Thomas gave the matter some serious consideration before he asked the all-important question, "So, what did *he* have to drink?"

Chapter Three

Now according to *Normal Time,* a person would have to say Darrel was two weeks late on completing the painting job, but according to *Savannah Time,* which is *Slo-vannah Time,* he was finished right on schedule.

Slo-vannah Time cannot be measured by two hands rotating around a dial. *Slo-vannah Time* is more like a state of mind.

When people first come to Savannah, they find it endearing that the people are so relaxed, unassuming, and polite. They don't mind waiting for meals to be served in restaurants, or for their hotel linens to be changed. They don't complain that the person walking in front of them on the sidewalk is walking slower than anyone thought was humanly possible.

Visitors liked experiencing *Slo-vannah,* until they needed something done quickly, like getting a car repair or trying to leave town. Then, *Slo-vannah Time* became a problem. That person who was walking so damn slow on the sidewalk was the same person who was now working on their cars.

Welcome to *Slo-vannah.*

Darrel, however, did appreciate the time it took to do a good job. He moved his paint brush over the last section of haint blue on the front porch. He ran the brush carefully against the trim on the front door. He had avoided painting this section, over the doorway, because he knew: when the last bit of haint blue was gone, there would be no barrier to keep out unwanted spirits.

He was not usually superstitious. He did not throw salt over his shoulder and he had walked under his fair share of ladders, but there was something about painting over haint blue that disturbed him. As his partner, Thomas, had said: It just wasn't right.

He stopped painting and looked at the final blue spot. It was an unusual shade. A spectacular color choice being not too blue and

not too green, and he should know what a nice haint blue looked like, being a painter and all.

There was a small loose paint chip dangling in the corner. He reached up, took it off and put the paint chip in his shirt pocket. He would save it and maybe use the color again, for a different job.

With a bold swoop of his brush Darrel covered up the last bit of haint blue on the three-bedroom house on Jones Street.

A slight shiver crossed his shoulder and up along his neck. He dismissed the notion that something, or someone, had rushed by. It was the breeze. Yes, it was most certainly a cool breeze on a hot Savannah afternoon. That swooshing noise that sounded like a wind being sucked beneath the door was just his imagination.

It sounded like someone, perhaps Thomas, was in the house, but Darrel had the key and the house was locked. Thomas should be on the back porch, hopefully cleaning up the drop cloths and ladders.

"Thomas, where are you?" Darrel called out.

No answer.

"Thomas!"

No answer.

Darrel climbed off the ladder and walked down the steps with his paint bucket and brush. He figured Thomas would help him clean up. Where was he? Darrel called out again.

Thomas did not answer, but loud noises came from inside the house and Darrel ran to the backyard to see what the hell Thomas was doing.

He collided with Thomas who was running around the side of the house towards the front. They looked at each other as the noise inside the house became more threatening.

"What's that?" Thomas asked with big eyes.

"That sounds like *let's get the hell out of here*, that's what!" Darrel said in a strange, nervous whisper.

They packed the painting cloths, ladders, brushes, and paint cans into the back of Darrel's truck. They sped out of *Slo-vannah Time*, they moved beyond *Normal Time*, they moved faster than greased lightning, and they zoomed down Jones Street like a couple of northerners from New York City — *Yankee Time*!

Chapter Four

Isabel Hurlander moved into the cute little white house on Jones Street with her two children. She came to Savannah for a nursing position at Saint Joseph Chandler Hospital.

They'd moved in on Saturday with the fresh coat of white paint only two weeks on.

Rebecca, the oldest girl being twelve, got first choice of bedrooms. She picked the larger room in the back because she liked the view of the garden.

Sandy picked the room across from the bathroom and as far away from the spooky, droopy, moss covered live oak tree that she could get. She was ten years old. She hated Savannah. She was too far from her father, who showered her with toys because he felt guilty about leaving them for his administrative assistant.

Isabel's room was at the front of the house and her window looked over the street. She hoped, in time, she would become indifferent to the tour trolleys that seemed to go by every half hour.

On the day they moved in, she found herself annoyed, not only with the tours, but with her daughters—and also with herself. What was she doing in Savannah? What had she been thinking to move so far from her friends and family? What if she needed help? Who would help her?

The movers seemed to take all day unloading the moving van. It should have taken half that amount of time. Isabel did not know about *Slo-vannah Time*. She was from Atlanta.

It was ten o'clock at night before she finally sat at the kitchen island counter with Rebecca and Sandy to eat a take-out pizza. The girls were sullen and ate mostly in silence.

After dinner, Sandy put the dirty paper plates, paper cups, and pizza box in the garbage and Rebecca put the left over pizza in the stainless steel refrigerator. The girls went upstairs to bed and

Isabel spent the next two hours emptying boxes and filling up the kitchen cabinets. She went to bed at twelve thirty, physically and mentally exhausted.

It was two in the morning when the noise started.

It was two-thirty when Isabel carried a hysterical Sandy to the car. Rebecca ran behind them clutching her mother's purse, looking frantically over her shoulder.

It was three o'clock when Isabel, dressed in her bathrobe and the girls in their pajamas, checked into the Hyatt Regency on River Street.

It was eight o'clock in the morning when Isabel called the lady at the rental agency and yelled at her for renting her a house that was haunted. She wanted her deposit and first month's rent back. No, she was *not* being irrational. No, she would *not* calm down. No she did not care about legal ramifications. The house was haunted, dammit! Click. Call over.

It was a little past one in the afternoon when the movers stood on the front porch at the house on Jones Street. No one was home. The front door was wide open. The lady on the phone said they should pack everything up and bring it to their new place on Wilmington Island.

Lucas did not think it unusual that he and James had moved the lady in yesterday and today they were moving her out. Strange things happened like that in Savannah all the time.

Lucas stepped into the parlor and looked around. James removed the baseball cap, worn backwards, off his head and scratched his scalp.

The men were too young to remember the 1940 hurricane that blew 150 mph winds through Wright Square, but they figured the damage had looked comparable to something like this.

They cautiously stepped over what looked like a once-upon-a-time coffee table and went into the kitchen.

The kitchen had suffered no damage. Oddly enough, the cabinets and drawers were closed, the contents inside neatly stacked and undisturbed. A dish towel remained neatly folded on the granite countertop, unaffected by the hurricane force winds that had blown through the rest of the house.

Of course, it did not explain how three slices of pepperoni pizza managed to get stuck on the kitchen ceiling.

"Lady said to pack everything up," Lucas said.

"Most of it is junk now," James observed.

"Humph. That it is. That it surely is. You start upstairs and I'll start in the parlor."

James adjusted his backwards baseball cap. "How long ya think it will take us to pack up this mess?"

Lucas gave it some consideration. "Day or two I guess."

James nodded in agreement. They were on *Slo-vannah Time*.

Chapter Five

The minute she walked up the steps of the quaint little house on Jones Street, Melinda Davenport loved it. She did not care how much the rent was, because her husband handled the money. She only *spent* the money and she intended on spending plenty of it to fix up this house.

She tucked Lord Pankerton, a little white Shih Tzu, under her right arm and followed the rental lady from room to room. Their heels almost seemed to click in unison across the floorboards.

Melinda peeked into the kitchen and said a polite, "Very nice appliances." She had no interest in the kitchen because she had no interest in cooking. She planned on dining out and, in fact, she had reservations at The Olde Pink House that very evening.

Melinda loved the backyard garden. She placed Lord Pankerton down by the stone bench under the enormous live oak. The tiny Shih Tzu was dwarfed beside the huge branches, wide trunk, and the streams of spooky gray Spanish moss.

Lord Pankerton looked up at the massive tree and shivered. He peed right there where he stood. (It was not unusual for Lord Pankerton not to control his bladder, though. Because of inbreeding and early abuse at the puppy farm, he was slightly retarded.)

Melinda signed the papers and wrote out a check. She came back for Lord Pankerton and put him into her big tote bag next to the rental agreement.

She couldn't wait to tell Bradley that they were now officially *Savannahians*. She did not care if he liked the house or not. She loved it!

Bradley did not care one way or the other about where they lived. After three years of marriage, he had given up thinking he might have an opinion. He sat on the back porch and watched the movers bring in all the expensive *crap* he had paid for, but never selected himself.

He *did* pick out the black BMW that he drove. Lucky for him the house on Jones Street, like most of the homes in Savannah, had a small gravel lane behind it and he was able to get his polished car into the backyard. (If Bradley had taken the trolley tour that passed by the house every thirty minutes, he would have known that the local folks jokingly referred to Savannah's back alleyways as the streets for the dead.)

There was no garage, but at least his car was off the street and would not be a target for thieves and hooligans. He wondered what the crime rate was in Savannah. Crime had not been bad in the Philadelphia suburb from where they'd come, but in Savannah, some people lived in gated communities.

He made a mental note to look up Savannah's crime rate on the Internet. He wondered where his computer was. The movers were working very slowly. A normal person would have finished the job hours ago. Bradley didn't know he had moved to *Slo-vannah*.

Melinda came out the back door, put Lord Pankerton down, and snuggled into the wicker chair to sit with Bradley.

"Don't you just love it here? The garden is beautiful, isn't it? Do you really need to park your car on the lawn? How *ever* did you get it through the narrow gate opening?"

"Talent my dear," he bragged.

"Well, I guess it is all right, since you will be at work during the day; but on the weekends, can you put your car on the street?"

Lord Pankerton peed on the porch.

Bradley hated the damn, stupid, retarded Shih Tzu.

"Oh Pankie!" Melinda cried and leaped to her feet. She rushed into the house and came out with a puppy pad. She placed it near Lord Pankerton and said, "Pankie, please do your little business on the puppy pads. This is our new home and we want to keep it neat."

Bradley wondered how much money they had spent on those 23x24-inch absorbent pads used to soak up urine. She had bought the dog a year ago. An impulse buy that he was still paying for: visits to the vet, special foods, little outfits, and enough puppy pads to go across Georgia — twice!

Lord Pankerton wagged his tail. He understood everything the woman said. She said, "*Mmm mm mmmmm mmm wwwaaww mmm sssssoooo mmmmm wawa mmm.*"

As the days passed in the new home, Lord Pankerton understood less and less what the woman said, but he understood what the shadows in the parlor said. They said, "Get out! No dogs allowed! Go away or you'll be sorry."

He sat in the kitchen and watched the shadows glide across the parlor floor. The shadows were always there and sometimes the woman and the man walked through the wisps of darkness without knowing it.

On the morning of the fifth day, when the man went to his car, Lord Pankerton did what the shadows told him to do. He ran through the kitchen, slipped between the man's legs and ran down the steps.

He tucked his tail between his back legs as he heard the man yell, "*WWWW MMMM DDDDaaammmit.*"

Lord Pankerton ran out the gate and into the street for the dead.

Melinda cried for two days. She put "Missing Shih Tzu" posters around the neighborhood, but Lord Pankerton was gone, never to be seen by them again.

Three days after the dog's disappearance, Bradley came home with a bouquet of spring flowers and a box of Godiva chocolates. He took Melinda to a nice restaurant for dinner.

They sat at a table for two and looked through the window at the occasional car driving down Jefferson Street. He ordered the Duck-Duck-Goose. She ordered the Diver Scallops. The waiter brought them their Shrimp Bisque appetizer, and then quietly disappeared.

Melinda stirred her spoon into the bisque and asked Bradley why he thought Pankie had run away?

Bradley did not know why a dog, who lived the life of a pampered king, would run away. But he didn't say that, instead he told her that her beloved dog would soon return.

"Do you think Pankie is all right?" She asked and tasted the delicious soup. She licked her lips with full appreciation for the flavor. The restaurants in Savannah were amazing!

"I'm sure he's fine. He's a smart dog," he lied.

"Lord Pankerton is so cute. I bet someone saw him and took him home."

Bradley could only hope that was true. "You know, I bet that's what happened."

"This soup is incredible. Don't you think?" she asked and then added, "Poor Pankie. He must be hungry. He needs his special foods, you know, or he gets sick."

Bradley knew all about Lord Pankerton's eating disorder. He really did not want to think about dog vomit at the moment. "I am sure the people who have him now know all about it."

God help them.

After dinner, they returned to the house on Jones Street. They had drunk a bit too much at the restaurant. Melinda drank in sorrow while Bradley drank in celebration.

They walked arm and arm up the stairs to their bedroom at the back of the house. Melinda kicked off her $300 designer high heels and fell on the plush king size bed. She lay on her back and watched the ceiling fan slowly spin over her head. It seemed to wobble. Funny, she never noticed that before. Perhaps she had too much to drink.

"Do you think Lord Pankerton is cold and lonely?" she asked, wiping away a small tear that was about to fall.

"No. I am sure his new owners are keeping him warm and well fed. Speaking of which, how about some cheese and crackers for us, and perhaps a small glass of wine?"

"Oh, okay. Will you go downstairs and get it?" Melinda asked.

Bradley went downstairs and into the kitchen. He pulled a bottle of red wine out of the wine rack and selected two wine glasses out of the cabinet setting them on the granite counter next to the bottle of red wine. He reached into the drawer for the cork screw, put it on the counter, and then stopped.

He wondered if she wanted red wine or white wine.

"You want red or white?" he called out.

Silence.

He took a bottle of white wine out of the rack and set it next to the bottle of red and the two glasses.

"Do you want red or white?" he called out again.

Silence.

He hummed a nonsense tune as he softly tip-toed up the heart pine stairs to ask her in person which wine she preferred.

Bradley stopped at the top.

Silence. Where was she?

"Melinda?"

Silence, followed by a long loud snore. Melinda was out cold.

Bradley leaned over and kissed her on the lips.

She opened her eyes, smiled, and asked, "What?"

"Do you want red or white?"

"I want another kiss."

Bradley smiled and kissed her again . . .

And then the noise started.

Chapter Six

Terrence was a Savannah cop. He had been on the police force for over seven years and could not remember the last time a donut had touched his lips. His wife was a physical education teacher at the high school and she would wrestle him to the ground if he did not maintain a healthy diet.

Terrence was lean, fit, and walked up the porch steps of the house on Jones Street with ease and grace. He had grown up in the Yamacraw Village Housing Project. He knew Savannah. He knew the people. He knew the feel of heart pine boards under his boot ...and he knew this house did not have a single spot of haint blue on it.

"Wut's up?" Terrence asked the pimple-faced rookie. The night shift always had the oddest collection of Savannah-Chatham Metro Police Officers, but he sort of liked them. They made his job interesting. Terrence liked things to be that way: interesting.

"Someone broke into their house," the rookie said. He tried to appear calm, but his eyes shifted around as if he might see a boogieman that needed to be shot dead.

It was two in the morning. All the boogiemen were asleep.

Terrence took a glance from the doorway into the parlor. It did not appear there was a single piece of furniture that had not been busted. "It looks like they wrecked more than they stole. Where are the homeowners?" he asked.

"Not homeowners, *renters*," The rookie corrected and then, by the glare he received, knew he had angered Terrence. The rookie swallowed hard. It was not a good idea to irritate your boss.

"So where are the *renters*?"

"On the back porch. They won't come in the house. They want us to check it out in case the robbers are still here."

"Did you check it out?"

"Hell no. I'm not going in there alone."

"Don't blame ya. There ain't no haint blue."

"What?"

"There's no haint blue on this house. Could be trouble."

"What kind of trouble?" the rookie asked and put his hand on his gun.

"Where you from?"

"Boise, Idaho."

"That explains a lot."

Terrence checked out the house for robbers and boogiemen, while the rookie made light conversation with the *renters* on the back porch.

Terrence had seen a good amount of burglaries, but this one took the cake for interior destruction. As he casually walked from room to room, he noticed the vandalism was widespread and consistent. Furniture demolished, closet contents thrown into the room, and drawers emptied. Knick-knacks broken and lamps busted. Pictures torn from the walls, and then discarded. The computer, televisions, and all electronics no longer functioned. Melinda's designer wardrobe was ripped to sheds. The bathrooms were not damaged and the kitchen remained untouched. The wine bottles, glasses, and cork screw were on the counter where Bradley had left them.

Terrence opened the back door and asked Bradley and Melinda to come inside to identify what had been stolen.

Since Bradley had no idea what they owned, the rookie walked with Melinda through the rooms while Terrence stood in the kitchen with Bradley and got the story on what had happened.

At about eleven, they'd returned from the restaurant. Bradley had come downstairs to get the wine, but had gone back upstairs

to speak with his wife. They were both upstairs when the noise started.

The thieves must have slipped into the yard when Bradley parked the car. He thought he'd locked the back door, but maybe not.

The house was ransacked in about twenty minutes. Bradley could not call for help because they'd locked themselves in the bathroom and he did not have his cell phone. They'd stayed in the bathroom for an hour, to make sure the robbers were gone, and then they'd come out of hiding and he'd dialed 911.

End of story. Or was it?

Terrence put his notepad down on the counter next to the wine. He was a beer drinker and not a wine connoisseur. But his wife enjoyed a good Bordeaux and he liked to impress her by bringing home a wine he thought she might like. He picked up the bottle of red wine. It was empty.

"Sir, did you drink some wine when you got home?" Terrence asked.

"No. I never opened the wine."

Terrence tilted the bottle and noticed the cork was snugly intact and wrapped with the paper seal. He picked up the bottle of white wine and it was the same thing: empty, but never opened.

He carefully set the bottles down, folded up his notepad, and glanced around the beautiful kitchen. For a moment, he thought he smelled the delicious aroma of a Georgia peach pie baking in the oven.

"I will send an officer by in the morning to take prints. I suggest you get a room for a few nights."

"Okay," Bradley said.

"You want a ride to a hotel?"

"No, I'll drive myself. I'm not leaving my car in this neighborhood."

Melinda and the rookie walked into the parlor and Terrence heard her say, "All my jewelry is here. Nothing is missing. This has been a horrible week. My poor little doggie was kidnapped three days ago and now we've been broken into."

Terrence thought, but did not say, *What do you expect when your house doesn't have haint blue?*

Chapter Seven

Miss Realtor clicked off her cell phone and tossed it on her desk. She didn't know why Bradley Davenport was so upset. Now they were going to rent a place in an exclusive gated golf community, *The Landings*, on Skidaway Island. Melinda could take up tennis and join The Book Club.

The house on Jones Street was becoming a real problem. The first renter said it was haunted, the second was robbed.

She needed help. She picked up her phone and called Pammie.

"Southcoast Rental," Pammie said on the other end.

"Hey, Pammie. How's it going up there in New Bedford, Mass?" she asked.

Pammie told her how it was going.

When Pammie was done, she told her about the problem with the Jones Street house.

"Got any colleges in Savannah?" Pammie asked.

"An art college and a couple of state colleges."

"Rent the house to college kids."

"You're crazy. They will trash the house. You remember how we were in college."

"Doesn't matter. That's what security deposits are for. I rent to UMASS Dartmouth students all the time. Here's how it works."

Pammie told her how it worked.

Miss Realtor placed the rental agreements in front of the college students. She was going to tell them how it worked.

"You each sign your individual lease to pay a third of the rent. Each of you puts down one third month's security for a deposit. You pay me every month on the first. If any one of you breaks the lease before the end of the year, you lose your security deposit. If one of you leaves and the other two stay, then it is the responsibility of those two to find someone to replace the person who left. If those two people do not find a suitable renter to take that person's place, then they pay that missing person's third."

It was pure genius! A win-win for the landlord. The place would be rented and, if anyone broke the lease, it was up to the students to find a renter. No matter what, she would get money. If they trashed the house, which was almost a guarantee, she would get the extra bonus of keeping the security deposit.

The three young women signed their individual leases that would end in one year.

They could move in immediately!

Annie wanted the large bedroom in the back next to the bathroom, but Shu-Yun took it. Shu-Yun did not speak English very well and when Annie tried to discuss it, Shu-Yun would say, "Wha?"

Annie gave up and took the front bedroom. She loved Savannah and did not mind the occasional tour trolley that passed down Jones Street.

Jenny took the bedroom next to Annie's in the front of the house. It had a small balcony that could be accessed by climbing out the window.

Shu-Yun was a Fashion Major. She moved in with her sewing mannequin, pins, threads, scissors, ribbons, and enough cloth to cover the state of Georgia — twice!

Jenny was a Fine Arts student majoring in painting. Almost every piece of clothing or furniture she owned had a splotch of paint on it that did not belong there. She came from the western part of the state and her father's father's father had fought and died in what Georgians referred to as *The War of Northern Aggression*, The American Civil War.

40

She did not hold it against Annie that she was a Connecticut Yankee. Jenny liked Annie and that was why she'd agreed to share the house on Jones Street with her.

Annie was an Interior Design major. She looked nice. She designed nice places for nice people. She was just too damn nice for her own good.

After unpacking all day, Annie and Jenny decided to go downtown to Congress Street and meet up with some friends. Classes started next week and students were gradually drifting back into town. They invited Shu-Yun to come, but she declined.

Jenny was the only one with a car. It was a battered Honda Accord that needed a tune-up and new tires. She was going to college on a full scholarship and unless she sold a painting, she was flat broke.

She backed out of the backyard, barely making it through the gate, and then turned the car onto the street for the dead.

Annie got out and closed the gate. Shu-Yun was home alone and she wanted her to be safe.

Jenny and Annie met their friends at a lively Scottish Pub. It was Thursday and open mic night. The singers had a country western twang, but that was not unusual for a Scottish Pub in Savannah. Before going home, they stopped in for a slice of pizza at a place on the corner of Congress and Whitaker Streets.

It was two in the morning when Jenny inched the car through the gates and into the backyard.

"This month's electric bill is going to be outrageous. Shu-Yun has every damn light on," Jenny said. The house on Jones Street was as bright as the Christmas tree on the White House lawn in December.

Annie turned off the lights as they walked through the house.

They found Shu-Yun in the upstairs bathroom crying, huddled between the tub and the toilet.

"Why you no like me? Why you come home make noise? Why you mean to me?" Shu-Yun sobbed.

"We just got home," Annie replied.

"Why do you have every damn light on, you crazy lunatic?" Jenny asked.

"Don't call her that," Annie scolded.

"Why not? She doesn't understand much English."

"I think everyone understands that. It's universal."

"Why you call me names?"

"See? I told you," Annie said, and helped Shu-Yun to stand.

Shu-Yun was not thankful. She pushed past them, stomped into the hall, and shoved open her bedroom door. "Why you so mean? Why you do this?" she yelled.

Jenny and Annie looked into her bedroom. Their eyes went wide in amazement, their mouths dropped open. It was the most remarkable thing they had ever seen! Absolutely incredible!

Jenny ran to get her camera.

The sewing mannequin was completely covered in pins and needles. Every inch of its soft human-like, headless, armless, legless form had a sharp point stabbed into it. The pins and needles were perfectly spaced and at an even depth. To complement the eeriness of the mannequin was a pair of scissors jammed into where the heart would be.

Shu-Yun bent down on her knees and began, at the bottom of the mannequin, to meticulously remove one pin at a time and place it into her little bead-covered pin box.

Jenny began to click pictures with her camera.

"You go away. I not like you. I move out. Tomorrow I go," Shu-Yun said. She jumped to her feet and slammed the door in their faces.

Jenny went into her room, crawled out the window on to the little balcony, and began to look through the digital images. Annie followed and huddled with her in the small space.

It was a lovely warm Savannah night. Somewhere someone must have put a Georgia peach pie on a window ledge to cool. The aroma was delicious.

"These shots are fantastic!" Jenny exclaimed and held the camera out to Annie. "This one is the best. I'm going to paint it, or something like it."

Annie looked at the blue-gray mist at the left top corner of the image. The lighting in the room had been poor, but the light on the pins and needles made them glow like sharp, silver daggers.

"Do you think Shu-Yun will move out?" Annie asked.

"Who cares?"

"Our rent will increase if we don't get another roommate."

"Get real, Annie. This is Savannah. There are college students everywhere. We'll have a new roommate in no time at all."

Chapter Eight

Jenny stopped at an art supply store to buy a canvas and some paints. Then she went to the college student center and stuck a "Roommate Wanted" sign on the board. From there, she went to her studio space at the Fine Arts building and began to paint.

When she finished, four hours later, her professors were impressed. Her fellow students were jealous and amazed. She packed up and headed home just as her cell phone rang.

"Yes, come on by and see the room. I'm on my way there now. Yes, that's right Jones Street. I'll meet you in twenty minutes," Jenny told the prospective roommate.

The Digital Animation student moved in on Sunday. He arrived with enough electronics, wires, cables, computers, flat-screen televisions, and gizmos to launch a rocket. Taking over the bedroom that once belonged to Shu-Yun, he sat in his control chair at his desk and proceeded to create a universe separate from reality. He closed the door, came out only to attend classes, and rarely spoke to Jenny and Annie.

They liked it that he rarely spoke to them. They thought he was weird. They called him Mister Techno behind his back.

Jenny and Annie told their friends about him as they sat at the outdoor café on Broughton Street. According to local rumors, when the café was renovated, human remains were found beneath the basement floor, but the coffee was great and no one in Savannah paid much attention to the dead.

Annie sipped her green tea and Jenny told their friends about the time Mister Techno's entire hard drive went blank and he lost his project.

"He blamed me. He said while he was sleeping, I climbed into his window from the tree in the backyard and I messed with his computers. He said I erased his hard drives and ruined his

animation project. Can you believe it? What a nut job." Jenny laughed and took a drink of her coffee frappuccino. "I wasn't even home!"

"He was really mad," Annie added.

"Yeah. I don't know what is crazier: that he would think I would know *how* to erase his hard drive, or that I would actually climb up the tree to do it!" Jenny laughed and everyone laughed with her.

"Mister Techno has been alone in his room for two days. We should go home and check on him," Annie said.

It was midnight. Jenny and Annie stood in the backyard and looked at the intense glow coming out of Mister Techno's window. It was bright enough to entice any passing alien to come in for a rooftop landing. At times, a blast of blue light flashed and almost blinded them. The rest of the house was dark.

"Damn, he's not much on energy conservation is he?" Jenny remarked.

"Mister Techno is an energy pig," Annie agreed.

"I'm going to tell him to shut it down," Jenny said.

Mister Techno had blown a fuse and they didn't know where the fuse box was to turn the lights on, so they climbed the stairs in the dark. For some reason, the staircase felt chilly, as if something quickly rushed by them and stirred up a cool breeze.

At the top of the stairs, they heard a digital voice saying, "It's Howdy Doody Time. It's Howdy Doody Time" over and over.

"It must be his animation project," Annie whispered.

Under the door crack they saw flashes of red, green, and blue lights.

Jenny knocked.

No answer. She knocked again.

"I bet he has his headphones on and can't hear us. Just open the door," Annie said.

Jenny opened the door, and then ran to get her camera. She would shoot this on a low F-stop to capture Mister Techno losing his mind.

He ran across the room from one computer to another. He could not stop the digital song, "It's Howdy Doody Time... It's Howdy Doody Time," from playing over and over. He swiped at the air in an attempt to grab the wires that spun around him. The wires glowed and switched colors from red to blue to green. It appeared the electronics were trying to capture and control him!

Jenny and Annie watched Mister Techo run back and forth to the shelves of blinking warning lights. He turned knobs and pushed buttons in a wild attempt to stop "It's Howdy Doody Time" from playing over and over and over.

By the crazed glazed look in his eyes, they thought the continuous playing of the song was about to explode his head.

Jenny clicked photos until Annie told her to stop. They crawled on the floor, under the cluttered desks, to find the power strips. One cord at a time they unplugged Mister Techno from his nightmare.

"It's Howdy Doody Time. It's How..."

And then silence.

Mister Techno plopped into his command chair. He sat in darkness mumbling softly, "It's Howdy Doody Time...It's Howdy Doody Time."

Annie called his professor. His professor called his parents. His parents came and boxed up his stuff. They walked Mister Techno, mumbling, down the front porch of the house on Jones Street.

On Monday, Jenny drove to the art store, bought a canvas, went to the student center, posted a new "Roommate Wanted" sign, and then went to her painting studio.

The first painting she had titled, *Pins and Needles*. She would title this one, *Digital Man*. It would have two images of a person who looked something like Mister Techno, split and going in two different directions, while luminous wires flashed around him and parts of his body faded off into a blue-gray mist that seemed to engulf him.

After six hours of non-stop painting, her professors called her brilliant. The other students were dutifully flabbergasted.

Jenny charged her camera battery when she got home to be ready for the next roommate.

Chapter Nine

They went through a series of roommates who never stayed more than a few days, maybe a week at the most. Jenny and Annie needed rent money.

Jenny took *Pins and Needles* to an Art Gallery. The gallery owner did not usually display new artists, but Jenny's painting was too unusual to pass up.

Jenny stood across the street in City Market and admired her painting displayed in the window. She wondered if this was what success felt like. She hoped so, because she was happy as a Tybee clam and soaring on cloud nine.

Her cell phone rang. It was her mother.

"Mom! You won't believe this, but I'm standing here looking at one of my paintings hanging in a gallery!"

"That's nice dear."

Her mother's wet-blanket voice covered Jenny's good mood.

"You used to paint such nice pictures of the mountains around Dalton. Everyone asks when you will come back. I am sure you can hang your paintings in Mountain Meadow Trading Post and I bet the tourists coming to see the Cherokee Indian sites would buy them."

"I'm in school, Mom. I won't be finished for another two years."

"You don't need anyone to teach you how to paint. You are so gifted, or at least you were before you went to that art college. What are they teaching you there anyway?"

It was useless to explain, so Jenny didn't bother. "I like the college Mom. I'm doing fine. I paint what I see and what I feel. It's what art is all about."

"Yes. That's why I'm calling. Your brother showed me photos of the paintings you e-mailed."

A bit of silence fell between them.

Her mother sighed, then continued, "These paintings are disturbing. Your father and I are worried about you."

Jenny knew that was not true. Her father was not worried about her. Her father worked at the carpet mill with her brother and everyone else in Dalton, Georgia. Her father worried about carpets.

"Come home, dear. Ralph Nasholds asks about you every time I see him. He is such a nice boy—so polite. You should have married him when you graduated from high school."

More silence between them.

The silence was long enough for Jenny's mother to know it was useless to get her daughter to change her mind.

"Well, dear. I know you're busy. I was just worried about you."

"I know, Mom. Thanks. Give my love to Dad and Steven," Jenny said. Steven was her younger brother.

"I'll tell Ralph you say hello."

"Yeah, Mom. You do that."

"Bye honey."

"Bye."

Jenny clicked off her cell phone and shoved it in her back pocket. She hoped her painting would sell fast because she needed the money.

Annie sat with her mother having lunch in the café on West Liberty Street. Annie ordered the Low Country Crab Cake. Her mother ordered the Cobb Salad. Annie planned on finishing her lunch with a dessert. She was going to take full advantage of a free lunch.

Her mother had flown in the prior night from Hartford, Connecticut. They'd spent the day shopping on Broughton Street. Annie's mother bought her some new outfits and now her lunch. In the morning her mother was flying back north.

Annie knew there was an ulterior motive for her mother's visit. This was not just an "I miss you; let's go shopping trip."

Her mother wanted to see what kind of house her daughter had rented. Was it in a safe neighborhood? Was it clean? What were the roommates like?

Annie gobbled down the crab cake, sucked some sweet tea through a plastic straw, and said, "Isn't this café great?" It was more of a statement than a question.

"Yes. Very arty," Annie's mother commented. She looked around at the student paintings on the walls.

From her face, Annie could tell that her mother found some of them quite disturbing. But she smiled and looked at Jenny's artwork on display. Jenny had an entire wall just for her. Annie recognized every one of their old roommates in the paintings.

Deadline: the caffeine-addicted Graphic Design major who moved in with an espresso machine, a frappuccino machine, a coffee maker, a ton of imported coffee beans, and a bean grinder. They found her in her room completely zoned with *Deadline* scribbled across all her projects.

Plastic: the Industrial Designer who claimed he'd invented an eco-friendly compound for plastic molds. He was making an anatomically correct robot and used his own body to mold the parts with his secret ingredients. He'd started with his penis. It took three people from the Industrial Design Shop and the entire staff at Urgent Care, forty-eight hours to remove the mold. Thankfully, he'd never tell his secret mold recipe.

Dance Into The Insane: Performing Arts.

When Art Collides: Art History.

Dream Tunnel: Sculpture.

Oblivion Jumper: Equestrian Studies.

Electric Chair: Furniture Design.

The Box: Architecture.

Annie ate a huge forkful of the crab cake, and then noticed her mother moving bits of salad around with her fork. The truth of her mother's visit was about to be known.

"Why don't you come back to New England? If not now, then after the end of the quarter. You can transfer to RISD."

Annie had been accepted at Rhode Island School of Design and at this art college in Savannah. She'd chosen this one and did not regret her decision. "I like it here. The Interior Design department is one of the top in the country. My professors are great. The program is wonderful."

"But you're so far from home."

"That's what we have airplanes for, Mom. You're here aren't you?"

Her mother wiped her mouth, tucked her napkin on her lap, and said, "When you graduate, you'll come home." It was a statement, not a question.

Annie did not think this was the time to tell her mother that she was never going back to Connecticut. She wanted to live in Savannah forever!

Chapter Ten

Jenny got the call on her cell phone. A tourist had paid a ridiculous amount of money for *Pins and Needles*. The gallery said she could pick up the check and if she had anything to replace it with, they would like to display another painting.

She gave them *Digital Man*, picked up the check, deposited it in her account, and kept enough cash out to celebrate in true Savannah style.

After calling Annie to tell her the good news, Jenny picked up some buffalo wings from Wild Wings in City Market and a two-liter bottle of Coke, and then headed to the house on Jones Street.

She squeezed the car into the backyard, grabbed the bag of food, climbed the steps, and entered the kitchen.

"I'm home!" she shouted out to Annie and put the bag of wings on one of the stools at the kitchen's center island counter. "Annie! Wings are here!" she called again.

No answer.

Jenny went back to the car for the Coke. When she came back, the bag of food had been moved from the stool to the counter.

"Guess you didn't like that, huh Annie?"

Annie wasn't in the kitchen. Perhaps she was in the downstairs bathroom. It didn't matter; Jenny had forgotten to close the gate to the yard. She went outside and when she returned there were three plates next to the bag of wings on the counter.

"Who's here for dinner?" Jenny called out to Annie.

No answer.

Jenny put the soda in the refrigerator and then called to Annie again.

No answer.

Jenny bounded up the stairs to find her.

Annie was leaned over her drawing table with her ear buds plugging her into music. She bobbed her shoulders with the beat and sang along. She used markers to add a color wash to her drawing of a community center's interior.

Jenny tapped Annie's shoulder to get her attention.

Annie jerked in surprise, and then removed her ear buds. "You scared me!"

"Who's here for dinner?"

"I dunno. Who did you invite?" Annie asked.

"You put out three plates."

"What are you talking about? I didn't even know you were home."

"You came downstairs, moved the wings off the stool, because you hate when I do that. Then you put the bag on the counter and then you took out three plates."

Annie laughed. "You're losing it Jenny, and it isn't even the end of the quarter."

Jenny scrunched up her face and gave the matter some thought, and then slowly and carefully repeated, "I came in, put the bag down on the stool, went out, came back, and the bag was on the counter; I went out again, came back, and there were three plates on the counter next to the bag."

They exchanged worried glances.

"Someone's in the house," Annie whispered and grabbed the *X-acto* knife off her desk. She often used the sharp tool for trimming art paper, but now it would serve as a weapon of choice.

"What the hell are you going to do with that?" Jenny whispered.

"This is sharp."

"Yeah, for a circumcision maybe. I think we need...." Jenny looked around the room, picked up a three-foot metal T-square and headed downstairs with Annie following behind.

They slowly made their way down the steps, one carefully placed foot at a time. Annie clutched the razor sharp *X-acto*. Jenny waved the T-square. They moved down the hall, stopped at the kitchen entry, and peered in.

The three plates had been moved from the counter and were on the center island with the food bag and a stack of napkins.

"We should call the police," Annie whispered.

"What do we tell them? Someone snuck into our kitchen and set the table."

"This is really weird. What do we do?"

Jenny didn't know, so she didn't answer. She carefully went to the back door with Annie close behind. They looked out the door. Nothing. They went to the kitchen window and checked that it was locked. It was.

They turned and looked at the counter. The two-liter bottle that had been in the refrigerator was now next to the bag, the plates, and the napkins.

"I think dinner is ready. We should sit down." Annie said. She slowly sat on one stool. Jenny slid onto another one. They looked at the third empty stool and then to each other.

"Open the Coke," Annie said.

Jenny twisted off the cap. "We need glasses," she said.

Annie got up and went to the cabinet.

"Better get three."

Annie put a glass down in front of each place.

They sat in silence.

"Jenny. This is really creeping me out."

"Me too."

They looked straight at each other across the counter. At times they looked out the sides of their eyes to the empty place.

"Jenny. I want to leave."

"Me too."

"Do you have car keys?"

Jenny nodded.

"Do you think it will try to stop us?"

"I dunno."

They sat in silence. It seemed to last forever.

"On the count of three, run to the door," Jenny whispered.

Annie nodded.

"One."

They held their breaths.

"Two."

They looked at each other.

"Three!"

They dashed for the back door.

Chapter Eleven

They sat at in the bar on Whitaker Street with the photo of Robert E. Lee's somber face looking down at them.

Jenny took full advantage of her increased income from the sale of her painting. She ordered the escargot for herself, the mussels for Annie, and a bottle of *Sauvignon Blanc* for them to share.

Annie was finally beginning to calm down. Whatever was in the house on Jones Street had not stopped them from leaving. "Do you think it is a ghost?" she dared ask.

"Definitely. Most likely. What else could it be?"

"I dunno. One of our friends messing with us."

One of their friends entered the bar and waved a greeting. It was Fibers. No one knew her name, only her major, so they called her Fibers and she didn't seem to mind. With her came someone Jenny and Annie did not know.

Fibers introduced him as Scott, majoring in Historic Preservation. People called him Historic Preservation Scott, or just HP Scott. Fibers asked how they liked their new place and they told them about what had just happened in the kitchen.

"This is Savannah. I would put my money on a ghost," HP Scott said, and ordered a drink for himself and one for Fibers.

"Are you a ghost expert?" Annie asked.

"Nope. I've just lived in Savannah a long time. I've seen some strange things."

"Yeah, like what?" Jenny was doubtful anyone had seen anything as unusual as a bag of take-out buffalo wings moving around a kitchen. And although the curious behavior of their old roommates was a bit strange, she had no proof of it being anything more than imaginative art students going berserk. Happened all the time in Savannah.

"I've seen The Foot Sniffer," HP Scott proudly stated. His eyes gleamed as he took a drink and looked at them over the rim of his glass.

"Who is The Foot Sniffer?" Annie asked.

"A Savannah legend." HP Scott leaned in close to tell his story.

"I was a freshman when the upperclassmen warned me about The Foot Sniffer. I thought they were kidding. I mean it was just so bizarre. They said there was a guy in town who would creep up on you, and then offer you ten dollars to sniff your feet."

Jenny and Annie burst out laughing.

"Ah, so you don't believe it. Neither did I, until one night I was walking on Liberty Street. I had a pepperoni, mushroom, onion pizza in my hand. I turned down Bull Street and I was crossing through Madison Square when I noticed someone following me. I turned around to face him, thinking I would give the robber a face full of my pizza box. The guy reached into his coat pocket. I thought I was going to get shot, but he holds out a ten dollar bill.

"I knew right away who it was." HP Scott waved his hand, as if dangling paper money. "So I said, hey are you The Foot Sniffer?"

"Then what happened?" Annie asked.

"Nothing. He ran away."

"That's a lame ending," Jenny said.

"Yeah. How is your ghost story going to end?" HP Scott asked. Jenny and Annie had no idea.

"We need to do some research. Find out who it is and what it wants," Annie said.

"You need a Ouija board," Fibers announced, and then asked, "Where do you get a Ouija board?"

"I have one," HP Scott said. "Hey. I preserve old homes; you never know what you might find in the attic."

"Maybe skeletons in the closet," Annie added.

"Or ghosts in the kitchen," Jenny said. "If you want to find out how our ghost story ends, meet us at our place at midnight with the Ouija board."

"Why midnight?" Fibers asked.

"That's the witching hour," Jenny said.

"You watch too many scary movies," Annie laughed.

Robert E. Lee on the wall seemed to agree.

Annie set out the candles: two on the fireplace mantel, one on each end table.

"Is this necessary?" Jenny asked and adjusted her camera settings for low light to catch something in the dark.

"Yes. We need to set the mood," Fibers said. She turned off the lights in the kitchen. HP Scott turned off the lights in the parlor.

They sat on the floor around the coffee table. HP Scott took the Ouija board out of the box and set it in front of them.

The gold and black board looked creepy, with mystic symbols and letters. The words *No* and *Yes* were in each bottom corner. The triangular-shaped pointer, called a planchette, had a clear circle with a sharp metal point. A spirit would move the planchette to a letter, a number, or to the words *Yes* or *No*, to give a message from the grave. HP Scott placed the planchette in the center of the board.

"This is going to be trouble," Jenny sighed and looked at Annie.

"How do you use it?" Annie asked.

"Everyone puts the tips of their fingers on the pointer," HP Scott explained. "Both hands."

They did as HP Scott instructed.

Nothing.

They waited.

Fibers was bored. "Nothing is happening. I have an itch on my nose. Can I scratch my nose?"

"You have to concentrate," HP Scott said.

"How can I concentrate when my nose itches?" Fibers complained.

"I think we are supposed to ask a question," Annie stated.

"I think you're right. Someone ask a question," HP Scott said.

Jenny leaned over the board and, as if speaking into a microphone, asked, "Is there anyone here?"

... And then the noise started.

Jenny, Annie, Fibers, and HP Scott sat in an Irish Pub on Drayton Street. It was twelve-thirty. The place was almost empty except for the bartender and two people playing darts.

Their table top was completely covered with drinks.

They were shaken from the events that had occurred in the house on Jones Street. It took another thirty minutes before they began to calm down.

"That was incredible! Did you see the Ouija board fly into the fireplace, then burst into flames?" Jenny asked.

"It went like a rocket," HP Scott said.

"Up in smoke and then sucked up the chimney," Annie said, and then added, "I didn't know the fireplace worked."

"I think I stepped on what was left of the Ouija board on the sidewalk when I was running for the car," Fibers said.

"What was all the noise about?" HP Scott asked.

"It sounded like it came from everywhere!" Jenny said.

"It sounded like a tornado came through the house," Annie stated.

Although none of them had heard a tornado before, least of all experienced one, they all agreed that the noise was something like what they thought a tornado would sound like.

"It sounded like stuff being busted up," HP Scott said.

"Busted with a hammer," Fibers added.

"Oh, hell! My interior design project must be destroyed!" Annie sighed. "My professor will never believe me when I tell her what happened."

"What did happen?" Fibers asked.

No one knew exactly for sure.

"Did you take pictures, Jenny?" Annie asked.

Jenny nodded, and then looked through the images on her camera. What she saw startled and amazed her. She passed the camera around. After looking at the images, HP Scott quickly downed his drink.

"I think you should stay at my place tonight," Fibers said.

Jenny and Annie definitely agreed.

Chapter Twelve

Two days later, Jenny and Annie stood on the back porch. They peeked though the kitchen window and then looked through the door glass.

"I have to see what is left of my interior design project. It is due tomorrow. I might need to fix it," Annie whispered.

"Okay. Okay. Let's go in together. Hold my hand. Don't you dare let go!" Jenny said.

Together they entered the undisturbed kitchen. There was nothing on the counter because they had put everything away when they'd returned with the Ouija board. They went from room to room, and with each step, they became more and more discouraged. Everything they owned, although it wasn't much, was destroyed. Annie's interior design project was a crumpled mass of shredded paper in the corner of her bedroom.

"I'm going to fail!" she cried. "My mom is going to make me go to RISD!"

"Well that's a fate worse than death," Jenny said with a forced laugh.

They went downstairs to the kitchen and stopped in the doorway.

The bag of buffalo wings had been taken out of the refrigerator and was on the counter. There was a place setting for three, complete with napkins, glasses, and the two-liter bottle of Coke.

"Damn. I'm hungry. You hungry?" Jenny asked and sat down.

"Jenny. This is really weird," Annie said and sat across from her.

Jenny pulled out some wings and began to eat.

"How can you eat?"

Jenny stopped eating and said, "Look at it this way, Annie. The entire house is trashed except the kitchen. We come in here and we are safe. Not only are we safe, but taken care of. I mean come on Annie, it's like your home and your mom has dinner ready."

Annie looked at the plates, and then around at the bright modern kitchen. It did feel comforting. Reaching into the bag, she took out a spicy buffalo wing. She took a hesitant bite.

Jenny poured the Coke into their glasses and then stopped at the third glass, unsure what to do. "Do you think ghosts drink?" she asked.

"I dunno. Ask," Annie said.

"No way! Last time I asked a question, the house got blown apart." Jenny laughed and put the bottle down. She'd decided ghosts didn't drink.

"What do we do now?" Annie asked.

"Clean up this mess and get new stuff, I guess."

"What about a roommate? I think Fibers and HP Scott told almost everyone at the college that our place was haunted. We'll never find anyone to move in."

"We'll put something on the Internet. I bet we can get someone from one of the state colleges," Jenny said. She sniffed the air and asked, "Do you smell that?"

Annie sniffed, smiled, and together with Jenny said, "Georgia peach pie."

They needed help with the rent and they had no furniture. They were sleeping on the floor in sleeping bags. They borrowed two lamps, a dresser, a puffy couch, and a coffee table from friends. They were hoping a new roommate would come with furniture. It was frustrating.

A student stood on the sidewalk with her boyfriend. "I don't like it," she said.

"But you haven't seen the inside yet," Annie said.

"I don't need to go inside; I can tell all I need to know from standing outside."

"This is a nice neighborhood, if that's what you mean."

"No. I mean this house doesn't have haint blue. I won't live in a place that doesn't have haint blue." She turned to her boyfriend and said, "Come on let's go."

Annie watched the prospective roommate leave. She was feeling discouraged. She called Jenny to tell her the bad news. No roommate. No furniture.

"Why didn't she like the room?" Jenny asked.

"She didn't even want to see it. She said she wouldn't live in a house that didn't have haint blue."

"What is haint blue?"

"I don't know. She didn't look like an artist. I thought she said she was a business major."

"Oh well. Are you going to class now?"

"Yep. See you later. Bye."

Jenny clicked off her cell phone and shoved it in her back pocket. She wondered what color *haint blue* was.

Annie locked up the house and wondered as well.

Jenny pondered the importance of haint blue as she purchased a bag of pretzels out of the vending machine. She passed by Angelica's studio and peered in. "How's it going Eeka?" she asked.

"Fine," Angelica answered. Her friends called her Eeka, short for Angelica. She sat on a stool in front of a 30x36 inch canvas. Her painting style was not like Jenny's, but they respected each other's work. They were both on full scholarships.

Eeka had lived in Savannah all her life, only leaving one summer to attend classes in France. She had paintings on display in a gallery on State Street and was on her way to becoming a successful low country artist.

Jenny plopped down in a chair, opened her pretzels, and offered one to Eeka, who declined.

"Another cultural statement, eh?" Jenny remarked about Eeka's painting. The wide brush strokes of color and textures gave an impression of two men shrimping in a tidal creek.

"Hmm. At least I don't paint eerie disturbing paintings like you. What's with the man hanging in space with fire, flames, and swirling streams of blue-gray mist trying to drag him up a fireplace?"

"I call that one *Mystic Mayhem*," Jenny said in reference to her latest painting; HP Scott during the Ouija board incident.

"I call it bizarre. I worry about you Jenny."

Jenny wasn't worried. She munched on her pretzels and looked around Eeka's studio. She noticed a repetitive theme and a distinctive use of color in the artwork. In each painting, somewhere, was a stripe of pale aqua blue. Sometimes the shade

and tint changed slightly, but there was always a touch of blue in Eeka's art.

"Ya know, I've never noticed this about your paintings before, but what's with the blue stripe?" Jenny asked.

"That's haint blue."

Annie knocked on Professor CW's door and was invited in. "Professor, this might sound like a ridiculous question, but what color is haint blue?" she asked.

Professor CW put her pen down, leaned back in her chair, and smiled, "No question is ridiculous. Haint blue is not a particular color. It can range from periwinkle blue to an aquamarine. In the past, the blue paint was a self-made mixture of milk paint formulas using lime and whatever paints were available. That is why the color varies. Since lime was a prime ingredient it was a deterrent for insects and birds. It killed insects. Lime is not used anymore in paints."

Annie knew that Professor CW liked her — even though the last project she'd turned in looked like it had been trampled by a herd of elephants. The professor seemed to prefer the creative and professional look that she usually displayed in her art. At one point Professor CW had implied that she believed Annie would graduate and be a successful Interior Designer.

Annie gave the matter of haint blue some thought, and then asked, "How is haint blue used?"

"Generally, on the exterior of a house, on the porch ceilings. I have seen it used on shutters, doors, window trim, and in extreme cases, an entire house. If you drive around coastal Georgia, South Carolina, and Florida, you will see haint blue."

"So it is a regional thing."

"More of a cultural by-product of the Gullah slaves brought here from Africa," Professor CW explained.

Jenny went to Eeka's painting and looked closely at haint blue. "What's the meaning of the blue? Why do you use it in all of your paintings?" she questioned.

"As you so often point out during class critics, I like coastal Georgia themes and I like to present my cultural heritage. Haint blue has connection to my roots."

"A symbol for water?" Jenny asked.

"Sort of," Eeka smiled an all-knowing smile, and then said, "It's voodoo."

"You're a voodoo princess!" Jenny laughed.

"I didn't say that. You did."

"What is the cultural significance of haint blue?" Annie asked Professor CW.

"The word *haint* translates as *spirit*. The blue represents water. It is believed by some that spirits cannot cross over water. If you apply haint blue on the entryways to your house it will keep the evil spirits out."

There was not a single spot of haint blue on their little house on Jones Street, not anywhere. It was ridiculous to believe in old Gullah superstitions, but it could explain the unusual events happening in their home.

Annie tried to sound nonchalant when she said, "Some people believe Savannah is haunted. That would explain all the haint blue in town."

Professor CW smiled and leaned forward, elbows on her desk. "I suppose it is all about what you *want* to believe," she said and then smiled.

"Blue Voodoo." Jenny jumped to her feet and went to each painting, placing her hand on the strip of haint blue. She had a great idea for her next painting and asked Eeka, "You wouldn't happen to be looking to share a house with someone would you?"

"Not with you. Your place is haunted."

"Awh, that's not true. Don't listen to rumors."

"Do you have haint blue on your porch?" Eeka asked and knew the answer by the look on Jenny's face. "Haunted. You need someone to clear out the spirits."

Jenny kind of liked the kitchen ghost. Even with ratty handed-down furniture, the place felt like home. The table was always set for them when they got home. Sometimes the house smelled like a freshly baked Georgia peach pie.

"I like our ghost."

Eeka was surprised. She put her paint brush down and said, "Spirits don't always play nice. They are trapped between two worlds. Sometimes they stay behind for vengeful business. You need to get that ghost out before someone gets hurt."

Jenny nibbled on a pretzel and remembered the way the house had been destroyed. Perhaps the lady in the kitchen wasn't as nice as she believed. Perhaps it was an evil spirit who wanted to kill her and Annie and keep their spirits locked in the house on Jones Street forever!

Jenny felt stupid, but asked anyway, "So how do I get rid of a ghost?"

"You need someone who knows about spirits."

"Like a Voodoo Princess," Jenny said with an amused laugh. This was getting completely silly.

"No, someone like my Grams, a Root Doctor."

Now it was totally absurd!

Chapter Thirteen

Grams lived on the south side of Savannah in Pin Point off the Diamond Causeway. Pin Point's claim to fame was that it was the childhood home of Supreme Court Justice Clarence Thomas. It was also the location of the once-upon-a-time thriving Pin Point Oyster Factory and, of course, where Savannah's local Root Doctor lived.

Jenny drove south on the Truman Parkway with Annie in the backseat and Eeka giving directions from the passenger seat. Eeka was also giving them a short history lesson.

"In the late 1800s, some African American slave descendants settled at Pin Point. The oyster shucking factory opened in the 1900s and brought jobs. It was a little community where everyone knew everyone else. Mostly Gullah. Did you know that the Gullah have managed to preserve their African language and culture?" Eeka rattled on.

"And lucky for us they know about ghosts," Jenny said, turned off the parkway and onto Whitefield Avenue, which was a small road heading towards the marsh.

"Spirits are serious business," Eeka reminded them. "So is JuJu magic."

"That's a candy," Annie said and laughed.

"No. A JuJu is a witch. They put spells on people. Sometimes they can control a person's mind, take over their bodies, and make them do bad things."

"Maybe that's what happened to our roommates," Jenny concluded.

"Turn here!" Eeka said as they approached the middle of nowhere.

Jenny drove into Pin Point: a small secluded neighborhood of trailers, single-story homes, and a long white building.

"That's the old oyster factory. They changed it to be a museum. They want to make this whole area a historical landmark. Stop. Go here. That's Grams' place."

Jenny stopped the car in front of a small wooden cottage accented with haint blue on the shutters and on the front door. They got out and walked across the crushed oyster-shell driveway.

Eeka knocked on the door. "Grams?" she called out. "You home?"

No answer.

Eeka called again, but there was no reply. "Sometimes Grams likes to sit by the marsh. Let's take a walk."

They walked to The Pin Point Heritage Museum and found Grams seated in a wicker chair watching the wind dance across the marsh grass.

Grams waved to her granddaughter. "Isn't this a school day? Shouldn't you be in class? I don't want to hear you've stopped going to school."

"Class is finished for today. I came to see how you were doing," Eeka explained and bent to give the old woman a kiss on the cheek and a warm hug.

"Well dear, as you can see, I'm doing just fine."

"I brought some friends from college to meet you," Eeka said. "This is Jenny and Annie."

Grams smiled in greeting, and then frowned. "Angelica, why did you bring trouble on my doorstep?"

"Jenny and Annie aren't trouble Grams."

"They sure are! They have trouble all around them like a black cloud. I don't mean to be rude, but Angelica, you take your friends, go away, and leave this old woman alone."

Eeka shrugged her shoulders. She knew there was no reasoning with Grams.

Annie was going to try. "We're sorry to be a bother...."

"Humph. That you *are* child, a bother."

"We thought you might be able to help us with our ghost."

"A ghost! In Savannah! Well I'll be. What a surprise." Grams laughed. "What do people expect when they build a town on top the dead? Can't be bothered to move the bodies, just figured they could move the headstones and that would be just fine. Go on they did and put streets, sidewalks, houses, stores, and restaurants on top of the dead."

Grams shook her head with disgust. "And there are a lot of dead here. Yellow Fever, wars, pirates killing folks, and then there's just the usual murder and nonsense killing going on. I expect there are some people that died someplace else, but maybe visited our fine town when they were living and decided to come back here instead of passing on. Savannah is such a friendly town like that. So, what kind of spirit do ya figure ya have visiting?"

"A kitchen ghost," Jenny said. "Usually she's nice, but sometimes she gets upset and destroys the furniture."

"And she sort of makes our roommates go crazy," Annie added.

"You don't say?" Grams sounded interested.

"Can you help us?" Annie asked.

"Well, I would like to, but I'm eighty-five now and I thought I'd give up root doctoring and let the young people take over. You can find out just about anything and everything you need on the Internet these days. Even a man! I expect you could find out how to rid yourselves of a spirit by looking it up on the Internet."

A slight breeze blew across the marsh and the saw grass moved as if in an orchestrated dance. Behind them the sun was starting to set. The vast barren marsh took on a golden orange hue. An eerie blue-gray haze formed in the distance.

"Grams you know about spirits more than anyone. Can't you help them? I mean, not only help Jenny and Annie, but help the restless spirits, too?" Eeka asked.

Grams sighed. "It's a heavy burden to put on an old woman. I guess if the Lord gave me this knowledge, he must expect me to use it for the good. Use it to help the living and the dead as well. Okay, I will do as the good Lord asks, but like I said, it is a heavy burden for an old woman to bear." She rose out of the comfortable wicker chair and said, "Let's get this business settled quick. I want to be back home in time to watch my ball game on TV. You got a car?"

Chapter Fourteen

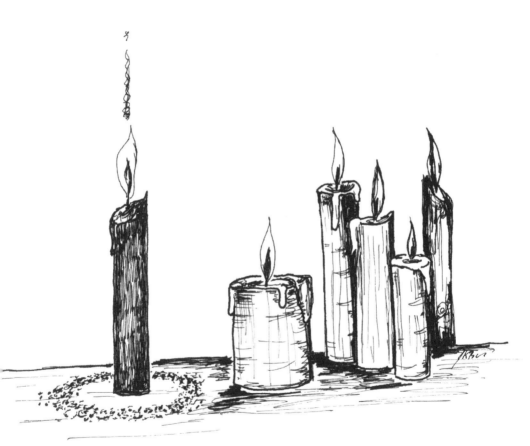

They had expected Grams' magic root bag to be decorated with mystic symbols or skulls and crossbones, but she came out of her house carrying an old red cosmetic case.

"That's your car? That ain't no kind of decent car. A car should be a Cadillac or you might as well call a taxi," Grams complained as she climbed into the backseat. "Will we be driving past a place that makes hamburgers? I haven't had my supper and I am gonna be hungry."

"We can stop for a burger. No problem," Jenny said and headed the Honda Accord, that should have been a Cadillac, back to Savannah.

They cruised through a drive-thru burger place on Victory Drive. The people worked in *Slo-vannah Time*. After twenty minutes they were back on the Truman Parkway with Grams happily eating a burger, fries, and sipping on a Dr. Pepper.

Jenny drove through Savannah to Jones Street, but did not park in front of the house; instead she squeezed the car through the gate into the backyard. "We're here. We'll go into the kitchen."

Grams got out of the car and looked at the pretty little house. "What do you expect? Not a drop of haint blue anywhere. No wonder you have a spirit. I expect you'll have quite an infestation once the word gets out," she said and, with Eeka's arm for support, started up the steps.

Jenny hurried ahead and opened the door. Annie followed everyone inside.

"Don't lock the back door. We might have to get out fast," Grams said.

Jenny, Annie, and Eeka sat on stools at the center island counter.

Grams opened her root case and peered inside. "Let me do all the talking. Y'all just sit there and don't say or do a thing. Ya hear?" she said.

They obediently nodded.

Grams took out an assortment of items and placed them carefully on the counter one at a time. She then asked, "I don't suppose I can get the blood of a virgin from any of you."

They exchanged glances and remained silent.

"Humph. I didn't think so," Grams chuckled. She was only fooling with them. "Guess I'll have to do without virgin blood."

She lit a stick of bright red incense with a match and walked around the kitchen in a clock-wise direction. "*Smoke of Dragon's Blood* to clear the room," Grams said. With the room filled with wisps of smoke, she then reached for a mayonnaise jar containing a fine white powder. She took a pinch and sprinkled it in each corner of the room. "*Protection Powder* to keep us safe," she explained.

Grams sat down, reached into her cosmetic case and removed four blue candles and one white candle. She placed a blue candle to the north, south, east, and west. "We ask for only kindness as we come with good intentions," she said, and then placed the white candle in the center. "Be restful. Be at peace."

Grams brought out a withered brown root and smiled fondly at her granddaughter and said, "*Angelica Root* to guard us against evil."

She unpacked a black candle and placed it at a safe distance from the others. "The evil spirit," she explained and then carefully brought out a plastic container. She opened it and sprinkled red-black powder in a ring around the black candle. "*Hot Foot Powder* to keep away spirits looking to cause us trouble."

Grams lit the white candle, the blue candles and the black candle. "We join hands, but Angelica you don't hold mine. We leave this opening for our spirit friend to come. We welcome the spirit to join us because we are a circle of friends," she said.

They joined hands as instructed.

"Now we wait," Grams said.

They sat silent in the kitchen. Time passed. It was *Slo-vannah Time.*

To Jenny, it was like sitting on a stone bench on River Street. She had all the time in the world to paint. A cool breeze soothed her as she painted her canvas. In the distance, a sailboat made its way under the golden structure of the Talmadge Bridge. Jenny could stay there forever, peaceful, rested, and happy. The Savannah River was a unique and beautiful shade of haint blue.

Annie sat in a brightly colored beach chair on Tybee Beach. The ocean breeze was a tropical wind that blew streamers of colored silk around her. The world was awash in colors, textures, and the most wonderful feeling of contentment and joy filled her heart. Annie wished to be nowhere else than sitting on the beach looking over an ocean of beautiful haint blue.

Eeka floated through the marsh creeks in a small flat-bottom boat. She painted the birds, crabs, and dolphins with her brush.

Her paper flowed with swirls of color that moved with the energy of the wildlife she painted. Life was full, rich, and wonderful. With a stroke of her brush, the tidal water turned into an enchanting haint blue.

Grams' eyes were closed. She nodded her head from time to time, sometimes wiping a tear from her eye, then shaking her head and giving a gentle smile.

They drifted peacefully in the kitchen of the little house on Jones Street for what felt like an eternity. It was comfortable and peaceful. The room was filled with the delicious smell of a freshly baked Georgia peach pie.

Eventually, Grams said, "Thank you ma'am," she kicked Eeka in the ankle.

"Thank you," Eeka quickly said from years of proper southern conditioning.

Jenny and Annie said, "Thank you."

Grams blew out the candles and collected her items.

"What did the ghost say?" Jenny asked.

Grams frowned and scolded, "It ain't proper to talk about someone as if they're not in the room when they are right here."

"Sorry," Jenny said and looked around into nothingness.

With her root doctoring collection back in place, Grams clicked the case closed and said, "We thank you for your hospitality. We'll do what we can. Good night, ma'am."

Jenny, Annie, and Eeka followed Grams outside. They stood for a moment on the back porch. There was a blue-gray haze under the large live oak tree in the garden.

"Go on now. You leave this place alone," Grams said and pointed an angry finger at a misty figure.

It could have been the wind. It could have been the television from the neighbor's house. It could have been their imaginations, but it sounded like someone was softly laughing.

Chapter Fifteen

Jenny drove down Jones Street to Price Street, and then turned right and headed south, out of town. Live oak trees lined their way through the forgotten streets of Savannah where tourists never visited. The town was somber and dismal. They rode in silence; each in their own thoughts.

Finally Grams spoke, "Miss Emma says your mammas raised you well. You are fine girls and she doesn't mind having you for company."

"That's our ghost's name, Emma?" Annie asked.

"Yes. Miss Emma apologizes for all your troubles, but she wants you to know it is not her fault. She does not like paper plates used in her kitchen and is sorry about throwing the pizza on the ceiling. She also does not condone excessive drinking and felt it necessary to empty the wine bottles. It is her house and she believes her guests should abide by her rules. She liked Lord Pankerton, the little dog, and hopes he is alright."

Jenny and Annie had no idea what Grams was talking about.

"Miss Emma has been in the house for a long time. She moved there in 1916 with her husband and their two children. Her husband signed up to fight in the war, that being The Great War, World War I. It was alright when he was at Fort Screven on Tybee and could visit them, but then he got shipped out.

"He was on *The Otranto* when it sank during a storm off the coast of Scotland in 1918. Three-hundred-seventy men died, hundred-thirty of them from Georgia. There are seventy-five unmarked graves in the military cemetery in Kilchoman Scotland, but her husband is not there. Robert's body was never found. Miss Emma doesn't understand why Robert, her husband, died. He was a good swimmer, having grown up around the Savannah River.

"Miss Emma had two young children to support. She started baking pies in her kitchen and sold them to people and to restaurants. At one time, she had three ovens in her kitchen and two women helping her. She was most famous for her Georgia peach pies. People came from all over for her pies. When President Roosevelt visited Savannah, he ate a slice of her pie and said it was the best he'd ever had. Yes sir, everyone loved Miss Emma's Georgia peach pies.

"In 1940, she died peacefully in her sleep in the upstairs back bedroom."

Jenny turned onto the Truman Parkway. They passed a broken-down brown truck on the shoulder. *Anything Painted* was painted on the driver's side door.

"Looks like Darrel ran out of gas again. That boy will never learn," Grams commented, and then continued her story.

"After Miss Emma died, her family rented out the house and it came into disrepair. It broke Miss Emma's heart to see her home falling apart around her. Miss Emma didn't want to leave her home. She isn't ready to move on just yet.

"Her family sold her house to a northerner who updated everything real quick to flip the house for profit. That's when Miss Emma got her new kitchen. She loves her new kitchen.

"The owners can't sell the house, so they just rent it out. They thought a fresh coat of paint on the porches might make the house easier to attract a renter. They painted over the haint blue on the porch ceilings and that was when the trouble started.

"There are a lot of spirits wandering the streets of Savannah. Most of them exist unseen among the living. It takes a lot of personal energy for a spirit to manifest in the living world. Often, all their hard efforts go unnoticed because the living are not

receptive to their messages. A living son might think the family photograph just dropped off the wall because of a bad picture hook, but it took days and nights of hard concentration for the mother to show her love from beyond.

"When spirits group together, they combine their energy and it is easier to cause events in the world of the living. Usually, they are up to mischief, which is what is happening in Miss Emma's house.

"When the haint blue was on the porches, other spirits could not enter her house and she could live peacefully inside. With the haint blue gone, it was like an open invitation for other spirits to come on in.

"Spirits with proper manners stayed away, but those looking to cause trouble came walking right up the steps and into the house. Miss Emma shoos them away, but sometimes they group together and she isn't strong enough to keep them out. That is when things get broken. Miss Emma stays in her kitchen until they go away."

Jenny turned off the Truman and they headed back towards Pin Point.

"Miss Emma said you should not let anyone stay in the back bedroom because there is a JuJu hiding up in the live oak tree. He is up to no good and gets into the room through the window."

They rode in silence, and then Annie asked, "Did Miss Emma say what we should do?"

"No. She is asking for your help to rid her house of unwanted guests," Grams said, and then asked what time it was.

"The baseball game starts in twenty minutes. You'll be home in time, Grams," Eeka said.

"How do we get rid of uninvited ghosts?" Jenny asked.

"I guess we could get a priest over for an exorcism," Annie said.

"But that might get all the spirits out and Grams said Miss Emma was not ready to pass over. We certainly don't want to throw Miss Emma out of her own house and into the street," Jenny said.

"Grams, why isn't Miss Emma ready to move on?" Annie asked.

"I didn't ask and Miss Emma didn't tell. It isn't polite to pry into other folks business," Grams answered.

Jenny parked the car and they all got out. Eeka carried Grams red cosmetic root case in one hand and helped steady her with the other.

"What do you think we should do?" Jenny asked.

Grams stopped on her front porch, thankful for the protective color of haint blue on her own door. "I think you need to put haint blue on the windows and doors. I think you should be careful when you do that. Spirits cannot cross over haint blue and if you put it on while there are unwanted spirits inside, they will remain in the house."

"But how do we make sure all the spirits, except Miss Emma, are out of the house?" Annie asked.

Grams chuckled and said, "Goodness child. This is Savannah. Throw a party. Everyone in Savannah comes out for a party, even the dead."

Chapter Sixteen

They put the word out: party Friday night. Everyone invited. Bring a friend. Bring your friend's friend. Free drinks. Bring a food dish to share. Party starts at nine and goes until whenever.

Jenny, Annie, and Eeka invited their classmates, their professors, the Deans, and the Department Chairs. They invited the college staff and extended a personal invitation to the college president. They invited their neighbors and they even invited their old roommates.

Every good party needs a theme. Everyone was asked to come dressed in a costume. The art college offered a variety of majors, including architecture, animation, performing arts, fashion design, and art history. The possibilities were endless and most definitely the costumes would be creative.

Guests would only be allowed on the porches, the front and back yards, sidewalk, and the street. No one was allowed inside the house. They made up the excuse that the house interior had been fumigated and unfortunately, not safe for bugs or humans. They did not mention ghosts.

Eeka was responsible for organizing the food, beverages, and guests. She set up food tables on the porches, coolers for ice and drinks, large garbage cans, paper plates, earth-friendly eating utensils, plastic to-go cups, and napkins. To ensure that no one needed to go into the house, she had a Port-O-Potty delivered and set up in the corner of the backyard. Guests could get from the front yard to the backyard by going down the small path along the right side of the house.

No one, under any circumstance, was to go into the house!

Eeka put white *Protection Powder* in a plastic baggie and tucked it in to her back pocket. Jenny mixed up a batch of haint blue. Eeka added Grams' *Hot Foot Powder* into the paint for an extra kick to

boot the spirits out the door. It was Jenny's task to paint the haint blue around the doors and windows to keep the spirits out.

Hopefully the spirits would be outside attending the street party. If not, it was Annie's job to find them, chase them out, or invite them out...or figure something out.

To do her part, Annie went to an antique shop and, for $2, purchased a 24-inch brass cross. Eeka said she thought crosses only worked for vampires, werewolves, and maybe undead zombies, but Annie said having a cross couldn't hurt. Jenny left the decision up to Annie.

Annie liked her cross and had it tucked under her arm as their party guests began to arrive.

They came from every department.

Fibers was dressed in a fully knitted green and yellow striped jumpsuit from head to toe, complete with a pointed hat and a bright pink fluff ball on top.

Two Architecture students dressed as Frank Lloyd Wright and the ancient Egyptian builder, Imhotep, arrived. They brought a block of cheese sculpted like the Guggenheim Museum in New York City to go with their stack of pyramid-shaped crackers.

Film students came as Charlie Chaplin, Zorro, and John Wayne. Two more students came as Orson Wells and Truman Capote.

Three Art History students dressed as Rembrandt, Vincent van Gogh (with a bandaged ear), and Salvador Dali brought a veggie lasagna. Students costumed as Georgia O'Keeffe and Pablo Picasso brought salsa and chips.

Four Fashion students, dressed in the style of the Roaring Twenties, brought an assortment of desserts that made fashion statements by being tastefully well made and presented with style.

Professor CW came with a hot shrimp dip and Bob from the model shop brought a platter of fried alligator. Deans from three

departments showed up and five players from the college baseball team.

The party was in full swing by eleven o'clock when the police showed up.

The rookie wanted to use the blue lights, but Terrence said it wasn't necessary. It was just a Savannah street party and there was no sense making a federal case out of it with sirens and lights.

Terrence stepped out of the car and surveyed the collection of weirdos. This town never ceased to amaze him. He told the rookie to wait by the car while he located the *renters*. Terrence remembered the house on Jones Street from a previous suspicious robbery.

Terrence walked up the steps and the rookie made light conversation with a student dressed as Marilyn Monroe in a tight sequined dress.

Terrence cautiously approached a young woman all knitted up in a bodysuit who was passing out plastic cups. "Who lives here?" he asked.

"Jenny and Annie," Fibers answered and handed him a drink.

"No thanks. I'm on duty."

"Are you a cop, or are you just dressed like a cop? You know, pretending."

"I'm the real deal. Can you show me Jenny and Annie?"

Fibers looked around the crowd, "Not here, maybe around back."

Terrence started for the front door.

Eeka stopped him. "Can't go inside. The house was just fumigated for bugs. Not safe," she said.

"Since when has this city allowed pesticides that are not environmentally safe?" Terrence questioned.

"Since this week," Eeka lied, but knew she had not fooled him. "Oh damn," she mumbled when he swung open the front door and stepped inside. She raced around the house, bumped into three students dressed as a sailor, a Native American, and Gumby.

Terrence walked into the parlor and noticed the lack of decent furniture. *College tuition must be killing the students,* he thought, walking through the kitchen and onto the back porch.

"Where's Jenny and Annie?" Terrence asked someone dressed as Leonardo da Vinci. Leonardo pointed towards the live oak tree in the yard.

One young woman had just finished painting a blue stripe around the tree trunk. The other young woman was banging on the tree with a cross and the student who had tried to stop him from going into the house was pointing at him. He tucked his thumbs into his belt and rocked on his heels. This was going to be interesting.

What was in the tree they were painting the stripe around? Perhaps an unfortunate art student with purple hair. He looked into the huge branches that dripped with moss. Among the darkness he thought he saw a slight movement, and then a branch seemed to morph into a black snake. The ominous snake changed into a wisp of blue-gray smoke seconds before it slipped into the open window onto the second floor.

The three apologetic art students stood at the bottom of the porch steps. Their faces worried and frightened. Terrence wondered if they were more afraid of him or of the blue-gray-misty-creature-thing he thought he saw. Then he noticed one of them holding a can of haint blue and he knew immediately what was going on.

"We better start with the upstairs. I saw something go into that window," Terrence said.

Chapter Seventeen

Terrence, Jenny, and Annie stood in the upstairs bedroom unsure what to do. Eeka was keeping guard outside the house, also unsure what to do.

"Are you the Savannah Ghost Police or something?" Annie asked Terrence.

"No. Savannah-Chatham Police. Here to protect and serve."

"Looks like you're going to have your hands full tonight," Annie said, and then added, "Thanks for coming officer."

"Terrence. Just call me Terrence."

"Lock up any ghosts before?" Jenny asked.

"Naw, but caught a lot of dudes who tried to disappear like ghosts. If there is a spirit in here, let's keep it here, at least for now. Put some haint blue around that window."

Jenny leaned out the window and began to paint a blue line around it. Annie held the paint bucket and held Jenny's arm to keep her from falling out. When Jenny finished, Terrence closed the window. They turned around and heard cackling laughter coming from inside the closet.

"It's in there!" Annie gasped and held up her cross.

"Whoa there!" Terrence stepped in front of the closet. "Let me check this out. You two stand back."

Jenny and Annie obliged and stepped back.

Slowly, carefully, Terrence reached for the door knob, but before he could touch it, the door burst open and a hot blast of air blew out and a gray-blue mist disappeared into the hallway.

"Quick paint a line on the floor at this door. The haint blue will keep it out of this room," Terrence said.

Jenny painted while Annie and Terrence stood watch. When she finished she started for the bathroom.

"Don't bother with that. Too much water in there. I think we have bigger problems," Terrence said. He cupped his ear and nudged his head towards Jenny's room.

Inside they heard children's laughter.

"Awh. Poor little children," Annie exclaimed and rushed inside before Jenny and Terrence could stop her.

The voices welcomed her with a rhyme, "Ring around the Rosie, pocket full of posies, ashes, ashes, we all fall down."

Jenny ran for the window and climbed out onto the small balcony. She started to paint around the window.

"Leave space at the bottom and we'll chase these little ankle biters out," Terrence said.

"They are only children. They need our help," Annie said and looked around in hopes of seeing one. "They sound so sweet."

"Yeah, sweet-evil-little-ghost kids," Jenny called from the balcony. In the yard below, she could see Eeka nervously watching her. The party continued unaware of what was happening inside the house. Six students dressed as The Addams Family discussed politics with three students painted like Blue Man Group.

The sweet-evil-little-ghost kids said another rhyme, "Nobody likes me. Everybody hates me. I think I'll go eat worms. Bite their heads off, suck their juices, spit their guts away."

Annie and Terrence exchanged worried glances. "You better hurry," Terrence said to Jenny.

"Fatty and Skinny went to bed. Fatty let go a fart and Skinny dropped dead. Fatty called the doctor and the doctor said, 'If Fatty let's another fart, we'll all be dead.'"

They heard a loud, long fart noise and then a green cloud appeared.

Annie gagged from the horrible smell. "I'm gonna throw up," she complained.

Terrence coughed and tried to hold his breath. "That's disgusting!" he moaned.

Jenny slipped into the room, immediately covered her nose, and asked, "What the hell is that rotten egg smell?"

"Quick, get the sweet-evil-little-ghost kids out!" Annie pleaded.

"How?" Terrence asked.

"Lizzie Borden took an ax and gave her mother forty whacks; when she saw what she had done, she gave her father forty-one," the sweet-evil-little-ghost kids chanted.

"I have an idea," Jenny said and stepped onto the balcony. She frantically looked around until she saw who she wanted. "Look!" She called back into the room. "I see Cinderella and look, there is Peter Pan and....."

In a sudden rush the sweet-evil-little-ghost kids swirled by and out the window. Jenny quickly painted up the window. Below she heard Peter Pan curse at Cinderella for knocking his arm and spilling his drink.

The sweet-evil-little-ghost kids were now loose on the town for a night of mischief.

Terrence and Annie waited while Jenny painted a blue line at the door.

They slowly advanced to Annie's room.

Annie peeked in and yelled, "Hey! What are you doing to my sleeping bag? Get out of my room!"

Terrence went in first with Jenny and Annie close behind.

"Stay in the center of the room. Don't let it corner you," he told them, but by the way Jenny and Annie clung to him he knew they were not going anyplace that he was not going. They shuffled to the window while the dark tornado cloud spun on top of Annie's sleeping bag.

It was not only her goose down sleeping bag that was in the cyclone, but all her interior design projects, her clothes, art supplies, and books. Annie was furious and swung the cross in the tornado's direction.

Jenny hung out the window and painted quick strokes as Terrence held onto her right foot. He had Annie by the arm. But with each swing Annie took and each brush stroke Jenny made, it was harder for him to hold them both.

"Get out! Leave my stuff alone!" Annie yelled and took a strong swipe at the cyclone's glowing red eye. "Ahhhhh!" she screamed as her cross was being sucked inside and she was almost dragged in.

"Hurry!" Terrence called to Jenny as he held on.

"I am painting as fast as I can. This isn't easy, you know."

"Yeah, but it's not the Sistine Chapel either; just make it quick."

"Help!" Annie screamed. The red eye seemed to grow larger, or was she just getting closer?

"Okay. I'm done. I left an opening. How do we get the thing out? What is it exactly, anyway?" Jenny asked as she slipped into the room.

The tornado ripped Annie out of Terrence's grasp. They helplessly watched Annie spin around in the tornado.

Annie yelled and smacked the red eye with the cross. Books, papers, and an assortment of art supplies swirled around her.

Terrence and Jenny tried to grab her as she spun by, but it was hopeless. Finally, Annie managed to grab the sleeping bag and cover the red eye. The tornado slowed down slightly.

Let's grab the sleeping bag and wrap this sucker up," Terrence said.

Annie jumped out of the slowly rotating tornado and helped them roll up what was left of the goose down sleeping bag. The spirit fought against them. They dragged it across the floor to the window. The bag started to rip.

"On the count of three, lift it up and throw it out!" Jenny said, "One....two....three!"

The sleeping bag ripped as they tossed it out the window. A cascade of white goose feathers filled the sky and spun around on a strong wind.

Laughter and delight came from the party guests below in the yard as they were engulfed in a whirlwind of feathers.

Jenny brushed on the haint blue to seal the window and painted a line on the floor in front of the bedroom door. When she finished, she inhaled a deep breath and looked at Annie and Terrence.

They wondered what waited for them downstairs.

Chapter Eighteen

They stood at the bottom of the stairs.

"Oh my God!" Terrence exclaimed.

"Frightening!" Jenny remarked with a shudder.

"Absolutely the worst!" Annie shook her head.

"Unbelievable," Terrence said.

"Terrifying," Jenny gasped.

"This is really scary," Annie quivered.

"GHOST TOURISTS!!!!" they said with a unified fear.

The room was full of out-of-towner-ghosts. They walked in a zombie-induced daze with their maps in hand and cameras hanging around their necks. They pointed at the ceiling and poked at the walls. They looked up the fireplace, gazed out the windows, and carelessly stepped on the furniture. Everything in their path was destroyed — smashed and busted to smithereens.

Their voices were an endless drone of questions: *Where is the Visitors' Center? Does the trolley stop here? Which direction is the Thomas-Owens House? Where is a good place to eat? Are you from around here? How far is River Street?*

The tourists were from different time periods and from a variety of different countries. A German with old-fashioned racing goggles was looking for the racetrack that once looped the south side of town. Two Girl Scouts searched for the founder of the Girl Scout's Juliette Gordon Low's home. A pirate, with a parrot on his shoulder, kept saying, "Where's me ship mate?" And the parrot repeated what the pirate said. A family of four from Cleveland, Ohio, was completely lost. A St. Patrick's Day partygoer, with a shamrock painted on his chest, stumbled about without spilling a drop from his plastic to-go cup.

It was the oddest collection of tourists that anyone could imagine. They faded in and out of existence and seemed to evolve into a huge mass of blended spirits.

"I've been dealing with tourists all my life," Terrence said. "I'll distract them. You hurry and paint the windows, but not the door. We'll show these visitors some true Southern hospitality."

Terrence walked boldly into the crowd. With his head held high and with a sincere smile upon his face, Terrence said, "Welcome to Savannah. Where y'all from?"

Jenny and Annie watched with complete admiration at Terrence's self-sacrifice, as he was immediately surrounded by a hoard of ghostly tourists only too happy to answer his question.

Kansas City. Toronto. Paris. Atlanta. Kenya. Montana. Springfield, Massachusetts. New Zealand. Miami. Amsterdam.

"Hurry!" Terrence called.

Jenny frantically painted the windows while Annie herded any wayward tourist back to Terrence.

The out-of-towner-ghosts started getting nasty. They pushed on Terrence and complained, *Why is everyone so damn slow in this town? I don't want to pay to park my car. Get out of my way! What do you mean Fort Pulaski closes at dusk? Don't you speak Dutch? You call this a cheese steak? Sweet tea is awful. The Georgia Bulldogs suck.*

"I'm done!" Jenny called.

Terrence escaped the crowd and joined Jenny and Annie at the front door. He held it open and said, "Thanks for visiting our fine city. Y'all can go on home now. Go back where y'all come from."

No one moved.

"Be good little tourists and go away," Jenny said.

No one moved.

"Street Party outside! Free drinks!" Annie announced.

The St. Patrick's Day reveler and the pirate hurried out.

"Y'all outstayed your welcome. Go outside," Terrence said in his mean cop voice.

The two girl scouts stomped out the doorway and threw a ghost box of thin mints at him as they left.

The room was still full of out-of-towner-ghosts that included three women from the Burlington, Vermont Camera Club, a Pittsburgh Steelers fan with his war paint on, a computer geek in town for an IT convention, and two hippies.

"This isn't working," Jenny said. "We need to entice them outside to the party." She opened the door wider and looked outside.

"Jenny what are you doing inside the insect fumigation house?" A student dressed as Batman asked.

"It's almost safe. Gotta get rid of a few more pests in here," she answered.

Annie came up with a brilliant idea. "I bet music will liven things up. Have some people out there sing. Everyone likes a free concert."

"Good idea!" Jenny agreed and called out for everyone to sing something.

"What do you want to hear?" A Performing Arts major asked, "A Broadway show tune?"

"Let's keep it simple. How about a Johnny Mercer song? Johnny Mercer grew up in Savannah. Everyone loves Johnny Mercer," Terrence remarked. He kept his attention on a suspicious-looking tourist carrying a suspicious-looking briefcase possibility full of suspicious contents.

Jenny asked the Performing Arts student to sing a Johnny Mercer song. She said she didn't know any.

"Sure you do. Sing 'Moon River'. No, I have a better one, 'Old Black Magic'!" Jenny said.

Annie and Terrence agreed that the song choice sounded perfect, given their situation.

The Performing Arts student began to sing.

"Jenny. It isn't working," Annie said. "They are getting bored."

"The tourists look restless," Terrence said. He opened the door wider, "The tour trolley is leaving now. Last chance."

The family from Ohio rushed out. The father clicked a photo of Terrence on his way past.

"Good riddance, y'all," Terrence said as he held open the front door. He looked outside and recognized three street performers from River Street at the party. He called out a hello to them.

"Hey Officer Terrence what ya doing inside the poison bug house?" Ray laughed. He stood with his friends. They had palm reed roses to sell to tourists tucked in their shirt pockets.

"Never mind, can you do me a favor and step up the beat to that song? Make it more… I don't know. Give it a River Street beat."

"Sure. Not a problem," Ray said, and grouped together with his friends as they worked out a song revision.

They started a beat and other people picked it up, tapping any object available, clapping hands, pounding chests and slapping knees, and adding mouth percussion until the music seemed to vibrate up and down Jones Street. Ray and his friends added the rap.

> Black magic goe'n slow, Got me feel'n blue and low
> Weave it black as night, can't stand up to fight.
> Icy fingers rip my heart, bleed my body and soul apart.
> Eyes cold as ice to me, hold back can't go free

The tourists started towards the door to see what the excitement was about.

> Noth'n 'cept Old Black Magic all the time,
> you cold mean witch waste my dime.

The tourists took up the dance beat and headed out the door.

Noth'n 'cept Old Black Magic all the time,
you cold mean witch waste my dime.
That black black magic... In your spell

The tourists went outside and mingled with the partygoers. They blended comfortably into the Savannah streets, only to be seen again, upon occasion, when other visitors least expected to see them.

With the last out-of-towner-ghosts out, Terrence slammed the door shut. Jenny painted haint blue around it. Annie swung the cross over her shoulder with a sense of great relief.

It was a relief they shared until they heard the dreadful cackling of someone or something laughing.

Chapter Nineteen

"I can feel some bad JuJu in here. It's in the fireplace," Terrence whispered.

But it was not there for long.

A huge black cloud billowed out, hung at the ceiling, and hovered over the three tiny insignificant humans.

The JuJu laughed. It was bad karma of unparalleled power in the form of negativity with the strength of Hercules. The JuJu seemed to have a face, somewhere in its shape, because it studied them, looking for a weakness, a vulnerable spot where it could enter their spirit to consume their willpower and control them.

The JuJu could make a person doubt themselves, hate themselves, and do things they normally would not do. The JuJu did this for its own amusement. It was the reason people failed to be who they aspired to be. It was the evil force that made people think: *I can't do that. I am not good enough. I am foolish to think I can achieve my dreams.* The JuJu made people believe these things, and when they believed it, the JuJu took control and made it so.

The JuJu was evil. The JuJu cloud of negativity headed for the kitchen.

Jenny rushed to the doorway and started to paint a line of haint blue. *I don't know how to paint*, she thought. *I am a stupid no-talent artist. I need to move back to Dalton and marry Ralph Nasholds.*

She stopped painting.

"What's wrong, Jenny?" Annie yelled. "Hurry! Don't let the JuJu get into Miss Emma's kitchen!"

"I don't know if this is the right color. Do you think it should have more green? Maybe white? I don't think I did this very well...," Jenny doubtfully said.

"Just paint the damn line!" Terrence used his cop voice.

Jenny painted the damn line, although she was not sure it was good enough, or straight enough, she forced herself to finish what she had started. She stood up, and admired her work. It was perfect! She was a good artist! Screw the JuJu!

The JuJu cloud flowed away from Jenny and swirled around Annie.

Annie held out her brass $2 cross and the JuJu laughed at her foolishness. She thought, *Everyone is right and I am wrong. A cross only works on vampires. Why am I so dumb? I've always been dumb. I am a silly girl with dreams of redesigning the White House. When I graduate I will move back to Hartford and live with Mom and Dad. I wonder if I could use this cross for... Wait a minute! I can put this decoration wherever I want. I know what I'm doing! I am right about this! I know it will work.*

Annie firmly held the cross up against the cloud. "Get back! Get out! Now!" She demanded and stomped her right foot hard on the floor just for added effect.

The JuJu chuckled at her antics, but knew it had lost. It moved back and slithered into the fireplace. The JuJu did not go alone, it pulled Terrence along, with every intention of dragging him up the chimney.

Terrence struggled, and when he realized he was going up front ways, he quickly turned backwards and braced his arms and legs across the fireplace. He was firmly set with his butt in the opening. He was able to stop from being sucked up, but the JuJu clawed at his arms and legs. It tore at his uniform and ripped off his left sleeve.

Terrence thought, *How the hell did I let this happen? Protect and serve my ass. My ass is stuck in this fireplace is all. I'm such a fool. What kind of kid thinks he can come out of the projects and make something of*

himself? Make a difference is all I wanted. I should have known better. Who am I fooling? Myself. Give it all up. Get myself a whole box of donuts and enjoy every last bite! Yeah, that's what I'm gonna do.

Jenny kneeled down and started to paint around the fireplace.

"Hold on Terrence!" Annie said and held out the cross to protect him.

Jenny had to paint around Terrence's outstretched body. It looked like a crime scene outline of a dead person, except it was a haint blue line and on the fireplace. The Savannah-Chatham Police Homicide Department would have a hard time solving that murder!

"My wife will know I ate junk food," Terrence said. "She'll figure it out. She's smart like that. Wonder why she married me? Always wondered about that. I don't deserve her. I don't deserve nothing."

With a final brush stroke, Jenny connected the line. She stood back with Annie and waited for the JuJu to stop clawing at Terrence.

"It's not letting him go. Why not?" Jenny asked.

"Lets pull on him," Annie said and together they each grabbed an arm and tried to help him, but the suction was incredible.

"She could have married that wanna-be-sweet-talking-lawyer. Money, jewels, a big house, and fame. Fame when he got caught with some dirty dealings in Macon. Yeah, my wife is smart. She must have seen through all that bull. I'm not like that. What you see you get. That's me. Honest. Good. Loyal."

The JuJu was losing strength.

"Helpful. Honorable. Faithful. A God-fearing good cop. Everyone knows it. I know it. And this damn JuJu is gonna know it when I kick some serious JuJu butt!"

The JuJu made a giant toilet flushing sound as it went up the chimney leaving Terrence behind.

They gave each other high-fives on a job well done. They laughed at their foolish thoughts. They were renewed with a sense of accomplishment and success.

But their joyful celebration ended abruptly when they heard Eeka screaming in the backyard.

Chapter Twenty

Terrence, Jenny, and Annie ran through the kitchen and saw Eeka's face outside pressed against the kitchen window glass. A huge dark cloud squeezed her. She struggled to escape, but pointed silver spears held her in place.

Jenny painted haint blue around the window. Terrence and Annie went outside to save Eeka.

Partygoers on the back porch watched in amazement. The group of Industrial Design students commented that the structure and durability of the window glass was quite extraordinary.

HP Scott thought the darkness around Eeka had an eerie resemblance to what had tried to suck him up the fireplace during the Ouija board incident.

He helped Terrence and Annie peel Eeka off the window glass. Eeka thanked them, rubbed her face, and was about to ask what happened when Jenny burst out the kitchen door.

"Hold the door closed! I have to paint around it!" Jenny yelled.

It took all of them to keep the door closed. It rattled, shook, expanded, contracted, cracked, and moaned. When Jenny finished painting, there was silence.

"What's going on?" HP Scott asked.

"Quite the show," a student dressed as Michelangelo said, and the next-door neighbor, dressed up like the next-door neighbor, agreed.

"There it goes!" Terrence said and pointed to what appeared to be a Georgia breeze stirring up paper plates and plastic cups.

But some people knew better.

"We need to get it out of the yard, close the gate and keep it shut while I put haint blue on the gate," Jenny said.

Their guests were being subjected to blasts of hot wind. A Performing Arts student in a queen's robe lost her crown. A furniture student vampire and a mummy-wrapped graphic design student, waiting in line outside the Port-O-Potty, were knocked against the fence.

"We need to lure it into the street for the dead," Terrence said in reference to the small alleyway behind the house used for service utility vehicles and garbage pick-up. Savannah was a neat and tidy town, even with its dead.

"How do we do that? How do we get the JuJu out of the yard?" Annie asked.

Eeka had the answer, "We need to offer a sacrifice!"

They stared at her, fearful of what she meant.

Eeka ran down the porch steps before they could stop her.

"Wait!" HP Scott said and ran after Eeka. "Don't do anything stupid! I know this thing, and it isn't very nice."

Eeka ran across the yard, through the harsh wind, and between the guests. She stepped into the alley and HP Scott caught up with her.

Immediately, the JuJu came after them. A dark negative cloud hovered over their heads. It prepared to descend to devour their spirits, change them into something they did not want to be.

Jenny ran out of the gate. Annie and Terrence held it shut from inside the yard while she painted the line of haint blue.

Eeka dug into her pocket and quickly sprinkled Grams' *Protection Powder* around her feet and HP Scott's feet. "Don't dare move out of this circle," she told HP Scott.

He had no intention of moving. The dark cloud swirled above them.

"Hurry!" Annie called to Jenny. "It looks really mad."

"Paint fast! I mean that! Paint really fast!" Terrence yelled as he saw the JuJu spinning towards the gate.

"Jenny!" Annie cried out.

In a panic, Jenny took what paint remained in the bucket and flung it at the iron gate.

Paint splattered on Annie and Terrence. When they stepped back they were striped in blue giving them a bizarre comical appearance. They looked at each other and hoped they did not look as stupid as the other did.

The JuJu rose up. It was what some people would mistake for a dark rain cloud on what otherwise was a clear Georgia night. Why the cloud hung over the house on Jones Street was odd, perhaps, but this was, after all, Savannah, and strange things happened here.

The wind blew. The thunder rolled. The lightning flashed. A loud crack of thunder shook the ground and a brilliant lightning bolt struck into the backyard. Guests shouted in amazement. The bolt struck dead center at the top of the Port-O-Potty.

All the negative crap was sucked up and gone in a rushing upward blast.

Annie and Terrence opened the gate and watched with Jenny, Eeka, and HP Scott as a dark whirlwind blew down the street for the dead.

They sighed in relief, but this time they were too stunned to pass out congratulatory high-fives. They walked into the yard in time to see a clown stumble out of the Port-O-Potty.

"Wow. That was intense," the clown said. His hair and face looking more disarrayed than usual.

With the JuJu and all the spirits out of the house, Jenny, Annie, Eeka, HP Scott, and Terrence went into the kitchen.

The aroma of a Georgia peach pie was so strong that Annie opened the oven door to see if anything was baking. Much to her surprise and everyone's delight, there was a pie inside. She used pot holders and brought it out. "Miss Emma must have baked it for us," she said.

"Smells good," Terrence remarked.

"Would you like a piece? I'm sure Miss Emma intended for all of us to have some."

"Sure would love to have some. Thank you very much."

Jenny got out plates and forks. She was mindful to set a place for Miss Emma.

"This pie is the best I've ever had," Terrence said.

"The crust is amazing!" Annie remarked.

"Fantastic!" HP Scott agreed.

"I've never eaten a sweeter Georgia peach pie," Jenny said.

"This pie is the best!" Eeka said and licked her fork.

"Thank you, Miss Emma, for this delicious pie," Terrence said, and then whispered to Jenny, "Who is Miss Emma?"

As they ate the pie, Jenny explained who Miss Emma was and what had been happening in the little house on Jones Street.

When she finished, Terrence said, "Well Miss Emma, don't you worry anymore. I'll drive by now and then to check up on things. Meanwhile," he said to Jenny and Annie, "I think this party is over. You are way past the noise ordinance cut off. Time for everyone to call it a night."

Jenny and Annie were not going to complain. They were ready to get rid of all their guests, the living and the dead. They announced that it was time to go home and the guests began to leave.

As Terrence walked to his patrol car, someone asked, "So the blue stripes on your uniform, you're dressed up like a documentary about life behind prison bars right?"

Terrence glared at the student dressed up like Willie Wonka and found it difficult to hide his smile. He thought, *This stuff only happens in Savannah.*

The rookie slipped onto the seat beside Terrence in the Savannah-Chatham police car. He was happy that the student dressed like Marilyn Monroe's phone number was secure in his shirt pocket. "You know, this was really a strange party," the rookie said.

"How's that?" Terrence asked.

"Well, some dude offered me ten bucks if I'd let him sniff my feet."

Only in Savannah.

Chapter Twenty-One

Darrel stood on the sidewalk with a can of haint blue in one hand and a paint brush in the other. The paint in the can perfectly matched the paint chip in his shirt pocket.

The young woman opened the front door. Her smile was gentle and sweet. "You must be the painter," she said.

"Yes Miss. Anything Painted. I'm Darrel and this is Thomas," Darrel answered, and then nudged his head to where Thomas struggled to get the ladder out of the truck bed.

"I'm Annie. Did the rental agency tell you what we needed painted?"

"Yes, Miss Annie. The lady said vandals put graffiti on the house. Sure does look a mess."

"There is some inside damage also, around the doors to some of the rooms."

"She didn't tell me about that."

Annie smiled, "Well, we didn't tell her that part. Don't worry I'll pay for any additional cost."

"Not a problem, Miss Annie."

"Is that haint blue in that can?" Annie asked.

"Yes, Miss Annie, and it sure is a nice color. I picked it out special just for this house."

Thomas came over to stand next to Darrel. His wide happy grin was infectious. "Picked the color out just for you he did Miss. Darrel is looking out for you. Don't you worry at all."

"Oh, I'm not worried. When do you think you'll be done?" Annie asked.

Darrel rubbed his chin, studied the puffy white clouds drifting overhead. His father always said, *wind from the east, fish bite the least, wind from the west, fish bite the best.* There was a slight westerly breeze on Jones Street. "Not more than a few days. Depends on

the weather." Darrel flashed one of those endearing southern gentleman smiles.

"That's fine. Let me know if you need anything. How about a bottle of ice water?" Annie asked.

"Well, will y'all just look at that," Thomas said.

They followed his gaze down the sidewalk and were surprised at what they saw. Walking with pride and determination a little white Shih Tzu strutted towards them.

"Awh. He's adorable!" Annie said.

Lord Pankerton held his head high and was unafraid. He had learned a few things about life by living on his own. He learned how to control his bladder, he was not a fussy eater, and he learned to survive. Some might think him slightly retarded, but it didn't matter what others thought because Lord Pankerton was the baddest, meanest ghetto dog in Savannah.

"Mighty proud isn't he?" Darrel said with a laugh.

Lord Pankerton strutted by Darrel and Thomas. He hopped up the front steps and clicked his nails across the heart pine boards. He went through the open doorway and past the door held open by the young woman. He lightly crossed through the parlor and sat down in the middle of the kitchen.

Lord Pankerton wagged his tail when the nice voice in the kitchen welcomed him home.

There are some who think Savannah is a city with old-fashioned southern charm. Those who live here know this to be true.

Grams told her hairdresser about Miss Emma and the house on Jones Street, who told her neighbor, who was friends with Kelly,

who worked at the Art Center. Kelly told Mark at lunch and he shared the story with the members of the gun club in Sandfly. Richard, at the gun club, went to church on Sunday and told everyone seated in the pew with him about the house on Jones Street.

Sam, the trolley tour driver, went to the same church as Richard. He added Miss Emma into his dialogue as he drove down Jones Street.

"Now if you look at that house with the pretty haint blue shutters and haint blue porch ceilings you might see Miss Emma baking pies in her kitchen. And if you do see her, it will be her ghost. Miss Emma died a long time ago.

"It is said Miss Emma's Georgia peach pies were the best in the county, no, the state, well, I hear they were the very best peach pies anyone ever tasted. Even President Roosevelt said it, when he had a slice of pie during his visit.

"Some folks say Miss Emma died at the hands of another baker who was jealous of her famous pies and gave her a recipe for death. We will never know why Miss Emma has not moved on to the other side, but what we do know is that, if you're lucky while you're visiting our fine city, perhaps you'll smell the delicious aroma of Miss Emma's Georgia peach pie coming fresh out of the oven."

The tourists sniffed the air hopefully. Some could smell Miss Emma's pies and some could not.

It is all in

what you believe.